KU-707-625

K A R E N   W A L L A C E

Climbing
a Monkey
Puzzle Tree

SIMON &
SCHUSTER

First published in Great Britain by Simon & Schuster UK Ltd, 2002
A Viacom company

This edition first published in Great Britain by
Simon & Schuster UK LTD, 2004
Copyright © Karen Wallace 2002
Cover imaging by Blacksheep © 2002 Simon & Schuster

This book is copyright under the Berne Convention.
No reproduction without permission.
All rights reserved.

right of Karen Wallace to be identified as author of this work has
sserted in accordance with sections 77 and 78 of the Copyright,
Designs and Patents Act, 1988.

YA
A852021
937

1 3 5 7 9 10 8 6 4 2

Simon & Schuster UK Ltd
Africa House
64–78 Kingsway
London WC2B 6AH

A CIP catalogue record for this book is available from the British Library

ISBN 0 689 83763 1

This book is a work of fiction. Names, characters, places and incidents
are either a product of the author's imagination or are used fictitiously.
Any resemblance to actual people living or dead, events or locales is
entirely coincidental.

Printed and bound in Great Britain by
Bookmarque Ltd, Croydon, Surrey

To Sam, with all my love

INVERURIE
LIBRARY
ACADEMY

One

"Where is Robert now?" whispered Caroline Bigfoot.

In the dark I couldn't see her face, but her voice was high and edgy. And I knew her hands were clenched under her sheets.

"He's almost at the top of Mount Everest," I said. "The snow is sparkling in the sun. The sky is bluer than you can ever imagine and there are mountains all around him."

"What's he doing now?" Caroline's voice was hoarse with excitement.

I swallowed.

This was the moment I had been building up to. I was telling the story of how Caroline Bigfoot's brother, Robert, singlehandedly conquered Mount Everest.

"He's unrolling the huge, heavy flag he has carried on his back all the way up the mountain," I said. I stopped for a second. I could see it all. The red, white and blue flag fluttering like a great bird. A young man standing beside it. His eyes were shining. His smile was modest and proud.

"Robert has done it," I told Caroline. "He's conquered Mount Everest."

In the bed next door to mine Caroline Bigfoot sighed. "I knew he would," she whispered. "Robert can do anything."

"Snazzy story, Nance," said Jenny Payne two beds along. "What colour was his snow suit?"

I thought fast. "Same colour as the flag, Jenny. Red, white and blue."

"Fab," said Jenny.

Beside me, Caroline moaned happily.

"I'm sick of hearing about Bigfoot's brother," hissed Rosalind Hunter from the other side of the dormitory.

"Yeah," muttered Sharon Downey in the bed next to her. "He's all she ever talks about. I want one about me marrying Cliff Richard."

"What about me and Princess Anne?" asked Rosalind Hunter. She sniffed. "I was going to her birthday party."

"Me first," said Sharon Downey. "I'm Dorm Head,

Nancy. I order you."

At that moment, boots clomped down the wooden corridor towards the landing outside our door.

Nurse Blessed was doing her rounds. And as she said herself, in her Glaswegian voice, which sounded like a rusty hacksaw cutting through plastic: *Woe betide the girl I find talking after lights out.*

We stopped talking and held our breath.

Nurse Blessed was short and square. Under her nurse's cap, she had a face that made a hatchet look friendly. I don't know how old she was but she must have been around 50 because her hair was the colour of wire wool. Nurse Blessed was almost frightening to look at. Her mouth was a mean slash in her face, and her grey eyes were the coldest things I had ever seen.

The boots clomped nearer.

I knew those boots. They were black and tightly laced, with short thick heels. They were also tiny and highly polished.

Nurse Blessed's boots reminded me of two blunt instruments.

Anyway, that night we were lucky. For a few

3

seconds, the shadow of her figure on the landing broke up the line of light under the door. Then she clomped away.

"Are you listening, Nancy?" hissed Sharon's voice. "I want a white satin dress and a big bunch of plastic roses."

"No one has plastic roses on their wedding day," said Jenny Payne. "Cliff'll think you're really stupid."

"No, he won't."

"'Course he will."

"So what should she have then, know-all?" It was Rosalind Hunter's voice.

"A cauliflower," said Jenny quickly. "Matches her face. Cliff'll love it, won't he, Nance?"

"You shut up, Jenny Payne," snarled Sharon. "Or I'll report you for talking."

"Shh," added Rosalind.

"Shh yourself," sneered Jenny. She turned over with a twang of bed springs.

In the dark, Caroline reached out and squeezed my arm. "Great story, Nancy," she whispered.

I plumped up my pillow and stared out of the window.

The branches of an enormous monkey puzzle tree glittered boxy and spiky in the moonlight. When I'd first seen it, the sharp-edged leaves reminded me of the newspaper firelighters my father had taught me to make at home in Canada. You tore up strips of newspaper and pleated them so they looked like square snakes.

That was when I thought a monkey puzzle tree was exotic and exciting. Then I got nearer and discovered that all the things I liked about trees you couldn't do with a monkey puzzle, because of its thorny leaves. You couldn't climb it because the leaves were so sharp. You couldn't make a rope swing because they wore down the rope. Even sunlight gave up trying to find a way through.

It was always dark and chilly around that monkey puzzle tree.

I plumped up my pillow again, and listened as one by the one the five girls in my dormitory fell asleep.

It was the moment I looked forward to every day because it was only time I could be on my own.

"Betcha there's no letter," said my brother, Andrew.

5

He slurped a mouthful of watermelon.

"Betcha there is," I said. I wiped the sticky watermelon juice from my face and rubbed my hand on my t-shirt. It was already covered in grass stains so a bit of pink juice didn't seem to matter.

We were sitting on a bench outside our log house in Quebec. Although it was almost the end of summer, it was still really hot, so the watermelon was cool and refreshing.

Andrew shrugged and blew a mouthful of pips a few inches from my face. "It's your turn to check the mail box anyway."

I looked at my bare feet. The track that led from our house to the mail box on the highway was covered in sharp chippings. You could cut your feet if you didn't go carefully. I knew I'd left my sneakers down by the swings behind the house. I always took them off when I went swinging because I liked to feel the wind between my toes.

Andrew was wearing socks as well as sneakers.

My mother's voice soared out of the window above.

"Will you two stop bickering and get the mail?"

Andrew and I looked at each other and took another bite of watermelon.

"Dad'll be home soon," muttered Andrew. "He'll do it."

I pushed the thready watermelon flesh through my teeth. More juice squirted onto my fingers.

"Shame to make the letter sticky."

Andrew looked at me. "Betcha there's no letter."

"Betcha there is."

"Jesus Christ!" bellowed my mother from inside the house.

We heard her footsteps on the stairs and ran up the track towards the highway. I stayed on the grass edges as much as I could.

I should tell you that my mother didn't usually swear like that. Well, not often, anyway.

The problem was that everyone was a bit edgy in my house that summer.

The reason for this was my grandmother. She was my mother's mother and lived in London. I used to send her stories I'd written, and one day, without asking anyone, she'd sent the whole lot to a boarding school called Woodmaston House, Moreton-on-Sea. With them she'd enclosed a letter asking the school to give me a scholarship.

Quite why she had done this I wasn't sure. Although the last time she had visited, I'd been eaves-dropping from my usual place at the top of the stairs and heard her talking about "hooligans" and "things going to the dogs".

My grandmother had a beaky face and wore winged lilac glasses. Her favourite colour was purple, so more often than not her dresses matched her nose. But one of the reasons I liked her was that we both shared a passion for dolls' houses.

And she loved buying me stuff.

On her last visit, she had taken me to Ottawa to visit a new toyshop that sold dolls' house furniture specially imported from England.

As Andrew and I walked up our track, I sum-moned up one of my favourite memories.

My grandmother and I were standing in the toyshop peering through a glass cabinet at a tiny but exquisite dining-room. There was a sideboard and a dining room table with six chairs either side and two carving chairs at either end. On the table were knives and forks, and rose-patterned plates smaller than bottle tops. Two silver candlesticks stood like miniature trees in the middle. A doll dressed in a velvet smoking jacket and looking very like my own Lord Marmaduke Mandeville, was sitting at the end of the table. He stared lazily at us with his knowing black bead eyes.

"D'you see those wee candlesticks, Nancy," whispered my grandmother. Her Scottish accent had softened with awe. "They've ones like them in the dolls' house at Windsor Castle. Do you not have a doll like this one in your own house?"

I nodded. "Almost the same, Granny. But Lord Marmaduke Mandeville spends most of the time in the kitchen."

"And why is that?" demanded my grandmother sharply.

"Because it's the only place he can sit down. I haven't got any proper tables and chairs."

My grandmother stared longingly at the dining room. "Och, Nancy. That'll never do. That'll never do at all."

It was a good day for Lord Marmaduke. By the time we left the toyshop, he could sit down anywhere he liked. He had the choice of the dining room, sitting room or study. Even the kitchen was newly furnished. The old stuff would do for the nursery.

So with one thing and another, if I did get the scholarship, the thought of staying for two weeks with my grandmother in her flat in London was not entirely disagreeable.

As for Andrew, the prospect of being on his own in Canada, virtually as an only child, was his dream come true.

We stood beside the highway looking at the rusty red mail box with our name on it. There was a dark slot where the letters were pushed in but no matter how I tried, I couldn't see if there was anything inside.

Andrew swung the key in front of my face.

"How much do you want to bet?"

A horn tooted. Our dark green station wagon pulled off the highway and stopped beside us. My father unwound his long legs from either side of the steering wheel and got out.

"Hi, kids." He looked at the mailbox. "Any mail?"

Andrew put the key in the lock and opened the door.

My knees went wobbly.

A thick white envelope with three purple stamps lay inside. *By Air* was typed in red on the top left-hand corner.

For a moment, nobody spoke.

"Well, it's what we've been waiting for," said my father quietly.

I couldn't look up at his face. We'd talked about me going away to school off and on all summer. He'd tried hard to hide it from me, but I knew he wasn't really happy about the idea. Of course, it was a chance to get a wonderful education, he said, but going away when I was barely 12 was maybe a risky thing to do.

At any rate, the conversation had always ended the same way.

"We'll find out soon enough, Buttons. There's no point getting all fired up."

Now my father picked up the letter and put it in

his pocket.

Andrew climbed into the front seat. I climbed into the back. The inside of my stomach felt like a beehive.

"I knew it was there," Andrew told my father.

He turned round and fixed me with his one of his cunning looks.

"Betcha they say no."

"You've won a scholarship, Buttons," said my father. "You're a smart girl."

He was sitting in his usual chair. Cigarette in one hand, a half-finished cup of milky coffee in the other. He took a long draw on his cigarette and closed his eyes.

Opposite him my mother put down her own cup of black coffee. "Listen, Nancy. You don't have to go if you don't want to. Granny won't mind."

But she was just trying to make it easier for me.

My grandmother would mind very much indeed.

And of course, we all knew that it was a once in a lifetime opportunity for me.

A couple of days later, as we poked about in the woods looking for interesting dead things, Andrew stopped and gave me a sideways look.

"You'll need skill and manage, Nancy," he said, as if it was definitely decided I would accept the scholarship.

He rolled over a rotten log and we watched hundreds of ants scurry for cover with their eggs clamped in their jaws.

"Skill and manage," repeated Andrew. "Like me."

"Wouldn't you miss me?" I asked. "I mean, there's nobody else around now."

Nowadays, Andrew and I were the only two kids who got on the school bus when it stopped on the highway at the top of the track. Our best friends Amy and Clare had gone to live in Ottawa when their mother married again. And the Wilkins, the only other family, had moved up north after their father got a logging job.

Andrew shrugged. "I've got stuff to do." He kicked the ground as if what he was about to say was something really difficult. "Anyway, you've got to think of yourself."

I didn't reply.

Maybe because it was pretty obvious that Andrew was really thinking about himself. But the truth was I had been thinking about myself, too. More and more the idea of going to the land where the Famous Five lived was taking hold in my mind.

Woodmaston House for Girls. Moreton-on-Sea.

I let the words roll around my mouth. They were fat and bursting with adventure, like English buns bursting with cream.

I saw myself with a band of friends. We'd ride bicycles along country lanes. We'd have picnics in flower meadows. We'd find clues in ruined castles and dig up sacks of Roman coins. And when we wanted a change, we'd jump on top of a red London bus and visit Buckingham Palace.

"Jesus Christ!" shouted Andrew who had taken up swearing as a full-time hobby. "Look at this!"

He was standing a few feet away from me under a maple tree. He pushed aside a pile of leaves with his foot.

"It's a squirrel!"

"Is it dead?"

Andrew prodded the ground with his foot.

"Yup."

"What kind is it?" I shouted.

"See for yourself," said Andrew in such a way that I knew it was a red one.

All summer I'd been looking for a red squirrel to make into a good luck charm. I'd even found the perfect gold chain for it at the local hospital Summer Sale.

My mother thought I was crazy. "Why can't you have a four leaf clover like everyone else?"

"Or a rabbit's foot?" suggested my father.

But the answer was no. I'd made up my mind. What I needed was a red squirrel's foot.

I ran over to where Andrew was standing and bent down to the ground.

A bright-eyed, tufty-eared red squirrel was lying in the leaves. It must have only just died because its rusty-coloured fur was still shiny.

I reached out to pick it up.

Quick as a flash Andrew's sneaker pinned down my hand.

"Uh, uh," he said in a sing song voice. "I found it."

He released the pressure of his sneaker by a fraction of an inch and smiled his cunning smile.

"But I'll give it to you if you promise to go to England."

I sat in a carriage on the train for Moreton-on-Sea and Woodmaston House. It smelt of old pipe smoke, new clothes and sick.

A girl opposite me with pigtails waved wildly to her mother and screamed, "Bye, Mummy! Bye Mummy! Bye Mummy!" As soon as the train left the station, she threw up over her brand new skirt. A lady in a uniform led the girl with pigtails away and another girl came and sat in her place.

"Hello," she muttered. "I'm Jenny Payne."

Jenny Payne had a full mouth, a Roman nose and a square jaw. She didn't look like a 12 year-old girl one bit. Later, when we got to know each other better, Jenny told me that when she was wearing make-up, she easily passed for 16. And by make-up, Jenny did not mean a hint of pink lipstick and a smudge of blue eye shadow. She was talking black eyeliner, bold white eye shadow and false eyelashes as thick and furry as tarantula legs.

Now Jenny and I sat in the carriage and watched each other curiously. We were the only ones who weren't crying.

I wasn't crying because although it was sad to say goodbye to my grandmother, her London flat was small and I knew that I was beginning to get on her nerves. Also I had said my real goodbyes two weeks before in a hot little room reserved for unaccompanied minors at Montreal's Dorval Airport.

At that time the prospect of the adventure awaiting me on the other side of the Atlantic kept my own eyes clear while both my parents were pale and drawn. And when the stewardess came to collect me, even Andrew couldn't bring himself to offer me a final piece of advice.

As for Jenny Payne, she told me she had only cried once in her life, and that was when her father was picked up in a big black car and taken to jail.

The thing I first noticed about Jenny was that even though we were both wearing stiff new uniforms (v-neck green jumper, a grey Clydella blouse, green ties with thin grey stripes, pleated grey skirts and knee-length green socks held up with garters), somehow Jenny had tamed hers.

Her pleated grey skirt was hoiked just that little bit too far up above her knees, while her oversized jumper was pulled just too far down over her backside. Her green tie was askew and her blouse was already crumpled. But the most thrilling thing was that she hadn't done up her top button so you could see the unmistakable glint of a gold chain around her neck.

The Woodmaston House for Girls' Official Clothes List was printed on four sides of yellow paper. At the bottom of the fourth page, written in italics, were the words, *All jewellery is strictly forbidden.*

Here was a girl I wanted to impress.

"I'm Nancy Cameron," I said.

Jenny wrinkled her nose. "Why do you talk funny?"

"I'm from Canada."

Immediately I had Jenny's full attention. She sat up and leaned towards me.

"Is that anywhere near where Elvis Presley lives?"

she asked in her low, hoarse voice.

All I knew was that Elvis Presley was American and America was next to Canada, but somehow I wanted to do better than that and in my enthusiasm I mixed up countries with neighbours.

"Yup," I said. "He lives next door."

Jenny's eyes lit up and she grabbed my hand. "Hey, honey," she said in the worst impression of a Texas drawl I had ever heard. "Can you and me be buddies?"

Pride and joy took off like twin rockets inside me. My great adventure was beginning at last.

With a screech of brakes, the train pulled into Moreton-on-Sea station.

Two

My lucky red squirrel's foot turned up trumps. Jenny and I were in the same dormitory. It was on the first floor, and it was called Dürer.

Not only that. Matron Goring, who was the Matron for my house, House One, even looked like a red squirrel. She had wavy reddish-brown hair, shiny chestnut eyes and while she didn't exactly jump from branch to branch, all her movements were light and graceful.

"Hey, kid," whispered Jenny as we stood in the hall, listening to Matron read out other girls' names and other dormitories. "That claw of yours is heap strong magic. Did you put it somewhere like I said?"

I nodded.

I'd shown Jenny my squirrel's foot on the train. She'd taken one look and told me to hide it as fast as I could. In her experience, bits of dead animal were always confiscated.

"Shh!" whispered a tubby girl behind us who had answered to the name of Sharon Downey. She had a mean mouth and cold piggy eyes. Her stringy red hair looked like limp bristles growing out of her head.

I didn't like the look of her at all and shuffled as far away from her as I could.

"There's your bed, Nancy Cameron," said Sharon Downey. "And that's your chest of drawers."

My lucky red squirrel had let me down. Sharon Downey was the head of my dormitory.

She pointed down the long wide room with five beds lined up on either side. Mine was the bed at the end, nearest the bay window. It had an iron frame and was covered in a pink candlewick bedspread. Five chests of drawers sat side by side in the bay window.

On one side of the room was an old fireplace and above it was a painting of a pair of praying hands.

"Jenny Payne, you're there," said a tall rubbery-faced girl called Rosalind Hunter.

I didn't much like the look of Rosalind Hunter either. She was deputy head because she and Sharon were second year girls.

"Matron says we can unpack," announced

Rosalind Hunter.

"Where's Caroline Bigfoot?" demanded Sharon Downey. She pointed a fat finger to the bed beside mine. "She's supposed to be here."

"Caroline's with Matron," said Rosalind Hunter. "She won't be a minute."

"Huh," muttered Sharon to no one in particular. "She'd better hurry up."

Caroline Swithins was a tiny girl with a wide serious face and pale green eyes. She wore the biggest sandals I had ever seen. They were like two tugboats on the end of her stick legs. Within minutes of meeting Sharon Downey, she had been renamed Caroline Bigfoot, and she didn't mind at all.

I liked Caroline Swithins and was glad I was next to her. As I dragged out the trunk that was underneath my bed, I smiled to myself. At least my lucky squirrel foot, now carefully hidden in my writing case, was trying as hard as it could.

An hour later, Matron Goring stood beside Jenny's bed and stared at the clothes that were stacked in neat piles on top of the bedspread. "Dear me, Jenny

Payne," said Matron Goring in her tinkling silvery voice. Somehow she managed to sound kind and worried at the same time.

Jenny watched frozen-faced as Matron shook out the home clothes Jenny had unpacked from her trunk.

Most of them were black, purple, or black and purple. The skirts were shorter than anyone else's. The sweaters all had scooped, lacy or deep V-neck-lines.

"Dear me, Jenny Payne," said Matron Goring again. She peered through her half-moon glasses at a sack dress that looked like a shiny ribbed tube. It was black, of course, and edged with purple braid.

"I'm afraid your home clothes are totally unsuit-able for casual school wear. I shall have to write to your mother."

"I buy my own clothes," muttered Jenny in a cold voice.

"Do you really, dear?" said Matron Goring sweet-ly. She folded Jenny's home things into a neat pile and tucked them under her arm. "Then we will have to buy some other ones for you and put them on your school bill."

The whole dormitory went silent. Already Caroline, Jenny and I had realised that home clothes were really precious. Everyone was curious about everyone else's. Compliments were made and given. Questions were asked and answered.

"Wow! That's fab! Where'd you get it?"

"Fenwicks in Bond Street."

"Fenwicks! That's my favourite shop! My Mum takes me there all the time!"

The coloured skirts, sweaters and party dresses which came from home were the only obvious things we had that were truly ours and made us different from each other.

The idea of losing your home clothes was too terrible for words.

"I think Jenny's clothes are lovely, Matron," said Caroline Bigfoot. "Please let her keep some." She walked over to Jenny's bed and stroked a fluffy black Angora sweater as if it was a kitten. "Jenny will be sad if you take them all away."

A strange expression flitted across Matron Goring's face. It was as if she was thinking about something in the past and trying to reach a decision about something happening now.

She reached out and patted Caroline Bigfoot lightly on the shoulder.

"You're right, dear. Of course she will be," said Matron Goring. She took the parcel of clothes from under her arm, peeled off a ribbed sweater and a stripy skirt and handed them back to Jenny. "And we can't have that, can we, Jenny dear?"

Jenny opened her mouth to say something, but as far as Matron was concerned, the case was closed. She turned and picked up the Official Clothing List that lay on my bed.

I knew there would be no problem with my home clothes. They were all made of paisley patterned vyella or green corduroy, and the nearest I got to fluffy black Angora were three lambswool twin sets in pale yellow, sky blue and rusty tangerine. My mother had taken me to a wool mill in Ontario and chosen them for me. As for the style, there wasn't a sack dress or shirtwaister among them. They were all home-made, which meant full-skirted and tied back at the waist. Except for one Black Watch tartan kilt, which I'd chosen especially to wear on the plane to

London. My favourite character in the Famous Five wore a Black Watch tartan kilt and when I saw one at a department store in Ottawa, I made such a fuss that my mother eventually gave in and bought it.

I watched as Matron's pencil flew down the Official Clothes List. *24 white cotton handker-chiefs, six pairs of white cotton linings, six pairs of grey woollen knickers, four grey aertex shirts, four green games shorts, one lacrosse stick.*

Pages were ticked and turned over.

Everything was going extremely well.

Then Matron Goring turned to the last page.

One writing case containing one fountain pen, three pencils, one rubber, a dozen envelopes and 24 sheets of note paper.

And also – and this was the terrifying problem for me – one carefully hidden lucky red squirrel's foot.

I watched Matron's hand move in what seemed like slow motion towards the red writing case that shone like a beacon on my pillow.

"What a pretty writing case, Nancy," murmured Matron as she held it firmly in her clean, short-nailed fingers.

My heart thumped like a road drill.

I knew perfectly well that if Matron found my lucky red squirrel's foot, she would say it was dirty and smelly. And I would never see it again.

And if that happened, I was sure everything in my new world would go wrong.

I stared across the room at the painting of the praying hands.

Sharon Downey had already told us as we unpacked our trunks that the painting was haunted.

Not only did the hands turn silver and twitch at night but Sharon swore that last year the hands had moved out of their frame and strangled a girl.

However, both she and Rosalind agreed that sometimes the hands made good things happen if you prayed to them hard enough.

As Matron fiddled with the zipper of my red writing case, I found myself staring desperately at the hands. Please, I prayed frantically. Please don't let her find my squirrel's foot.

The hands twitched!

A bell clanged through the house. "Tea time!" bellowed a voice.

Matron Goring signed my Official Clothes List and handed me back my writing case.

"Very good, Nancy," she chirped. "You may put away your clothes after tea." She spun on her feet and hurried out of the door.

"That was lucky," whispered Caroline Bigfoot. "Your secret is safe now."

I stared at her. "How do you know I've got a secret?"

There was something about Caroline Bigfoot.

On the coach ride from the train station to the school, I had been given a seat by the window. As the coach wound up through the town, I stared out at the rows and rows of huge houses that lined the leafy streets.

They all looked very tidy, very solid and very dark.

I thought about the school prospectus and the strange language which I had virtually learned off by heart.

Woodmaston House occupied an excellent position in Moreton-on-Sea. The town was·said to be one of the healthiest places for children in the whole of England.

I wondered where the unhealthy ones were.

Suddenly a whole paragraph leapt into my mind.

Only a short distance from the sea, the school stands about 200 feet above sea level on the old Burnham Road. There is little traffic to disturb children at work or in dormitories at night. The school buildings consist of three substantial and attractive houses which are interconnected and have been extended to provide classrooms, a laboratory, a domestic science room, a school hall and recreation rooms. The large playing fields are behind the school, where there is almost entirely open country.

Fifteen minutes later I found myself wandering alone across the grassy playing fields at the back of the school. There was no sign of entirely open country. At least not the kind of country I was used to.

Even in the towns in the Gatineau, you could see trees and fields stretching for miles and sometimes the glint of the huge Gatineau River.

The playing fields at Woodmaston House were surrounded by high wooden fencing that was too tall to climb over. I was shut in everywhere I looked.

For the first time since I waved goodbye to our wooden house in the woods, I felt homesick.

That was the moment Caroline Bigfoot appeared. To begin with she trotted beside me, her huge sandals flapping like clowns' shoes over the grass.

Then she said, "I feel safe with you."

And since she was, and since I was feeling homesick, I just smiled and we kept on walking. It was as if Caroline Bigfoot was a skinny, stray puppy who had decided to follow me.

Three

You had to wear overalls at all meals at Woodmaston House. They were brown, full-length with long sleeves and tied at the waist like a life jacket. When I first put one on, I thought it was just a practice run to make sure that we new girls knew how to feed ourselves without getting our entire bodies covered in gravy. Once this was established I was sure we would be allowed to take them off. Certainly wearing overalls seemed a strange way to teach girls table manners, which was one of the many undertakings made in the gold-embossed prospectus.

However, I soon realised that our overalls were to become a second skin. Because the truth was that they had nothing to do with learning manners or even basic eating skills. We wore overalls to keep the House's laundry bill down.

But as Jenny Payne pointed out after we had eaten half a dozen school meals, overalls did have their uses. They had two big pockets in the front and the school food was disgusting.

A few days after we had unpacked our trunks, hung up our games clothes and settled the one furry animal we were allowed to bring – in my case a monkey – on our beds, Jenny and I followed the herd of girls thundering down the corridors to the dining room. Well, it was called a dining room, but it was more like three long tables in a lean-to greenhouse.

"Bags sit next to Jenny." It was an expression I'd heard time and time again and I wanted to try it out.

"Sssh," hissed Sharon Downey in her now familiar, overbearing way. "Don't talk."

At the top of the table Nurse Blessed had been watching us take our places with a look of undisguised distaste. Even in these early days, most girls had already learned to keep out of her way. She jerked her head to one side.

"Who was talking?" she bawled.

Her voice cut through the scraping of 50 or more chairs.

"Please, Nurse, it was Nancy Cameron," said Sharon smugly.

Nurse Blessed pointed to one of two empty chairs

on either side of her. "Nancy Cameron, sit here."

Jenny patted my arm as I moved away.

Sharon Downey shot me a mean, triumphant look.

"And you, Sharon Downey, will sit opposite her," snapped Nurse Blessed.

The triumphant look disappeared. Sharon's flat piggy eyes glared at me. "I'll get you for this," she hissed as she followed me up the room.

I sat down beside Nurse Blessed and tried to avoid looking at her.

The more I knew her the more she reminded me of a dangerous dog. Nurse Blessed could bite you any minute, for no reason. If there were muzzles for people, she should have been made to wear one.

"Salt," said Nurse Blessed abruptly.

I passed her the grubby glass salt container and watched in amazement as she dumped half of it on her plate.

"Hasn't anyone told you it's rude to stare, Nancy Cameron?"

"Sorry, Nurse." I blushed scarlet. "Please, Nurse," I said, trying desperately to think of something to say to her. "My grandmother comes from Scotland."

"And why should that interest me?" asked Nurse Blessed.

She buttered a piece of fried bread and stuffed it into her slot of a mouth.

"If I wanted to talk to you, Nancy Cameron, I'd begin the conversation myself. Now finish your tea and stop prattling."

She got up from her chair and went to pour herself another cup of tea from one of the huge metal pots on the serving table.

"Never mind her," whispered Sharon Downey in a surprisingly kind voice. "She can be a right old witch if she wants to."

She passed me some more fried bread and picked up a jar of glossy brown stuff from the other side of the table.

"What's that?" I asked.

"Chocolate sauce," said Sharon. "It's for a special occasions only."

It didn't occur to me to ask what the special occasion was.

"It's really good with fried bread," said Rosalind

Hunter, who was sitting a couple of places down. "Try some."

"Thanks."

I took the last of the fried bread and put it on my plate.

Fried bread was a wonderful discovery. I'd never eaten it before and to me it tasted like Danish pastries, which I loved. I especially loved chocolate Danish pastries. At Woodmaston House there was always lots of fried bread but I hadn't come across chocolate sauce before. I took a big spoonful of the brown stuff Sharon had passed me, and spread it thickly over the triangle of fried bread.

Perhaps if I hadn't been thinking about Danish pastries so much, I would have noticed the way my end of the table had stopped talking. I might even have seen that some girls were nudging each other and giggling.

As it was the whole table went silent as I shovelled my newly discovered delicacy into my mouth.

The next second I couldn't believe what was happening to me.

The inside of my mouth caught fire and a sharp burning taste shot up my nose.

Tears filled my eyes and poured down my face.

What was this awful stuff?

There was only one thought in my head. I had to get this filthy muck out of my mouth as soon as possible.

I brought my regulation green napkin to my lips and spat a burning brown mouthful into the middle of it.

Which was the moment Nurse Blessed turned around.

"Nancy Cameron," she shrieked. Her eyes were furious and sharp as ice picks. "How dare you behave like an animal in my dining room?"

"Please Nurse," said a girl whose name I didn't know except she was also a first year. "Sharon Downey told Nancy that Marmite was chocolate sauce."

"I'm from Canada," I tried to explain. "We don't have Mar-"

"Silence!" snapped Nurse Blessed. She banged her fist on the table. "Leave this room immediately."

As fast as I could I stuffed my napkin into my overalls pocket and walked out of the dining room.

As soon as I was out of sight, I ran. On either side the corridors were a blur as I tried to fight back the hot tears that filled my eyes.

I couldn't understand Nurse Blessed at all. Almost from the moment I'd met her, she seemed to dislike me. At first I wondered whether it was my voice. Maybe my Canadian accent made me sound cocky and rude. Although lots of other girls in House One had funny accents because the school prided itself on being international – so there must be another reason. Maybe I was too tall. Or my eyes were too blue. Or my teeth were too crooked.

I could still feel her hands as she had yanked my mouth open during my first-day school medical examination. Her fingers felt like pliers.

"Tonsils?"

"I don't have tonsils, Nurse."

"Don't be ridiculous, child. All girls have tonsils." She yanked my mouth open even wider just in case I was lying.

The filthy taste of Marmite was still in my mouth.

I decided to try and find a washroom. At least I'd be able to rinse my mouth out with water. I turned down another corridor of sticky wooden floor boards and came to a black and white tiled hall. I couldn't find a washroom anywhere. And now I was lost.

Suddenly I began to cry.

A young woman, carrying an armful of books, appeared out of a doorway. I vaguely recognised her as one of the teachers who stood in a semi-circle at the front of the Hall during morning assembly, but she looked barely older than a sixth former. Instead of the usual teacher's box-pleated skirt and floral blouse with or without cameo brooch, the young woman wore a black and red stripy sack dress and with a big sloppy cardigan slung around her shoulders.

"I think the dining room is down that corridor on the right," she said helpfully. "I'll take you if you want."

I could only shake my head.

"But you'll be hungry if you don't eat lunch."

"I was sent out, Miss," I muttered.

"Ah."

The young woman bent down. "What's your name?"

"Nancy Cameron, Miss."

To my amazement, she knew exactly who I was.

"Nancy!" she cried. "I'm so glad to meet you. You're our Canadian story writer, aren't you?"

"Yes, Miss."

"I'm Eleanor Parkes," said the young woman. She smiled. "Miss Parkes to you, I suppose. I'm a student teacher and I'll be teaching you English and writing." She stood up. "I hope you will write me lots of stories."

"I'd like that," I said quickly. Then I felt stupid. I was learning to hide my feelings from teachers in case they got things wrong and used it against you. Now I'd let myself down.

Miss Parkes smiled. "I'd like that, too."

I looked into her face for the first time. She wasn't pretty, but her eyes were clever and kind. You got the feeling she could guess what you were thinking.

"You mustn't cry," she said gently. "You only feel sad because things are strange. Soon you'll have a lovely time."

She stood beside me for a couple of moments. It was as if she knew I didn't want her to leave me. I realised with a shock that just as Caroline Bigfoot felt safe with me, I felt safe with Miss Parkes. It was a shock because I didn't think I would need to feel safe with anyone.

Miss Parkes put down the books she was carrying.

"Why did you get sent out of lunch?"

I told her and afterwards she shrugged and pulled a face. "Sounds a bit unfair to me. Maybe you should try and keep out of Nurse's way for a while. I'm sure she's only bad-tempered because she's busy."

She picked up her books and we walked back down the corridor towards House One.

"You go that way," she said and pointed to a corridor I recognised.

I turned to her. I didn't know what to say but I wanted to thank her for making me feel better.

She put her hand on my shoulder. "Promise me something."

"Yes, Miss Parkes."

"If you're ever unhappy, come and see me."

"I promise."

Suddenly I had no problem finding my way. I

skipped all the way back to the recreation room.

Barely two minutes later a crowd of whooping, yelling, first years burst through the doorway and half pushed, half carried me across the floor.

It seemed I was not a troublemaker after all. I was a hero.

"Crazy bat," shrieked a girl called Barbara.

"I hate her," cried someone called Sarah. She dropped her voice. "I bet she knew what was going on all the time."

"Then why didn't she stop them?" someone asked. "I mean what happens if she doesn't stop New Girls' Treatment?"

There was a silence.

New Girls' Treatment.

It was what second years did to first years. It was a House tradition. You weren't a real Woodmaston girl if you didn't get given New Girls' Treatment. And getting tripped up or having your pocket money stolen was nothing. Some of the stories we had heard about New Girls' Treatment sounded as if they had come straight out of a medieval torture chamber.

The flushed faces around me turned pale.

"Of course she'll stop New Girls' Treatment," whispered somebody. "She's a nurse, isn't she?"

"If she won't, Matron will," said a girl called Deborah.

At the other end of the room, half a dozen second-year girls sprawled on the sofa and slouched over the cane chairs. When they heard us whispering, they put down their copies of *Bunty* or *Judy*.

"Lesley," said Rosalind Hunter in an extra loud voice. A girl with buck teeth looked up and grinned. "What do you think ever happened to Imogen?"

"Stupid name like that, she got what she deserved." said Lesley. "Anyway, no one should have hair that long."

"Why not?" asked a girl called Gillian, as if she knew already.

Lesley and Rosalind giggled.

"Because it blocks lavatories, that's why."

"At least she got her face washed," said Gillian thoughtfully.

"Stupid name, Imogen," muttered Lesley.

Rosalind looked up to make sure all the first years were listening. She needn't have bothered. You could hear a pin drop and at least two girls had tears in their eyes.

"At least Imogen wasn't fat," said Rosalind, spitting the word out of her mouth like a bit of gristle.

A girl called Christine joined in. "Are you talking about fat Fiona?" she asked sweetly.

"Fattest new girl ever," replied Rosalind. She looked as if she had forgotten something. "Whatever happened to her?"

They all looked at each other as if they were trying to remember something.

"I know!" said Lesley, laughing. "Someone wrapped her up in an eiderdown and tied her to a chair."

"Didn't they turn the heat up?" asked Rosalind in a vague voice.

"Yup," said Lesley. "But it didn't work."

"What didn't work?" asked Gillian, looking puzzled.

Lesley shrugged. "She didn't melt."

They picked up their copies of *Bunty* and *Judy* and began to read them again.

"I hope I only get an apple pie bed," mumbled a

new girl called Barbara.

"Not if they put sugar in it, you won't," said Jenny.

"What's an apple pie bed?" I asked.

"You'll find out," said a high, mean voice from the doorway. "I'll make you one specially." Sharon Downey swaggered towards me. "I might even put chocolate sauce in it."

"You leave Nancy alone," said Jenny fiercely. "Haven't you caused enough trouble already?"

"I was only trying to be helpful," said Sharon Downey. "Besides, you can't talk to me like that, Jenny Payne. I'm your superior, remember?"

"You're nothing," said Jenny in a flat bored voice. "You're just a big pig in a little pen."

It must have been something in Jenny's voice. Sharon went bright red and puffed up like a toad.

"I'm not nothing!" she shouted. "I'm not nothing!"

I could feel her brain working overtime. She stamped up to Jenny and kicked the leg of her chair. "I know something you don't know."

"Like what?" asked Jenny, ignoring the jolt of her chair.

Sharon stood up to her full height. She was about

as tall as a beer barrel. "I know what French kissing is!" She shouted out the words as if she were slapping down a hand of winning cards.

Jenny rolled her eyes. "Big deal," she said. "Everyone knows that."

At this point, I decided to join in the conversation.

"We don't have French kissing in Canada," I announced firmly.

To my surprise, Jenny looked at me as if I was off my head. "Of course you do, Nancy," she said quickly. She winked at me.

I knew somehow she was trying to save the situation but I didn't know what it was, or how it had even been lost. I decided my only way out was to stick to my argument.

I turned to her and spoke in my most serious grown-up voice. "We definitely don't have French kissing, Jenny," I told her. "You see, Canada is thousands and thousands of miles from France."

"Ha," crowed Sharon Downey. She turned to Jenny. "Your friend Nancy isn't as smart as she thinks she is."

She turned to me. "Come on, Nancy," sneered Sharon Downey. "I dare you to let me give you a French kiss."

I already knew what it meant if you turned down a dare. You were a coward. A weed. A sissy. I looked at Jenny.

"What should I do?" I muttered.

"Brace yourself," said Jenny. Then to my complete astonishment, she burst into uproarious giggles.

My crowd of admirers had now turned into a crowd of curious onlookers. I wondered if any of them knew what French kissing was.

I stared at Sharon Downey's shiny piggy-eyed face. She was much smaller than me but much wider. It occurred to me that if French kissing was anything like wrestling, I'd get the better of her pretty quickly.

I made up my mind.

"I'm ready," I said, clenching my fists into balls.

"Close your eyes, then," commanded Sharon.

"You never said anything about closing eyes," I said.

A smirk passed over Sharon's fat face. "You really are stupid," she said. She turned to the crowd that had now formed a circle around us. "You can't give a French kiss with your eyes open," she said in a matter-of-fact voice.

I closed my eyes, clenched my fists tight and placed both feet firmly on the ground.

"Okay," I said between gritted teeth. "Give me a French kiss."

And the next moment, Sharon Downey pushed her squirmy wet tongue into my mouth and I almost threw up.

That night I lay in bed and stared out of the window. The branches of the monkey puzzle stuck out like rigid snakes against sky.

How could so many horrible things happen to me in one day? It was almost as if Sharon and Nurse Blessed were determined to make my life miserable.

Even the thought of Miss Parkes didn't help. She was in House Two and that might have been the moon as far as I was concerned.

Andrew's words echoed in my mind. "You'll need skill and manage, Nancy."

Maybe he'd guessed something I hadn't even

thought of. As far as I was concerned, coming to school in England was going to be the great adventure with extra fun piled on top.

How wrong can you get?

I sniffed miserably and wiped my nose on my sheet.

"Don't cry, Nancy," whispered Caroline Bigfoot in the dark beside me. "Are you missing polar bears and icebergs?"

"I was thinking about my brother," I said in a choked voice.

"I think about my brother all the time," whispered Caroline Bigfoot. "He's fantastic."

I sniffed again. "What's his name?"

"Robert. He's tall and he's got curly hair just like you."

Boots clumped along the corridor towards the landing.

"One day you'll meet him, Nancy," said Caroline. "And I know you'll really like him."

The boots clumped nearer. The thought of getting into more trouble with Nurse Blessed made me feel sick.

"Shh," I whispered to Caroline as quietly as I could.

But there was no reply. She had already fallen asleep.

I felt under my pillow for the hard square of my writing case. As quietly as I could I unzipped the case and pulled out the length of gold chain. In the moonlight, I could see the delicate shapes of the squirrel's tiny claws. Its fur felt light and smooth in my hand.

"Help me," I whispered. I squeezed the claw gently and put it back in my writing case.

Immediately I fell into a horrible dream.

A pair of black lace-up boots followed me everywhere. No matter what I did, I couldn't get away from them.

"Get up and shut up."

Someone grabbed me by one arm. Someone else tried to drag me out of my bed. Something like a handkerchief was being stuffed into my mouth.

I bit the fingers fumbling between my teeth.

Sharon Downey gasped and pulled back her

hand. "You bitch," she whispered.

"I'll get the writing case," muttered Rosalind. "You pin her down."

Rosalind pulled at my pillow. I knew immediately that they were trying to steal my squirrel's foot.

I shoved myself up to the top of the bed so I was sitting on my pillow with my legs clear. I heard a soft thud as my toy monkey fell onto the floor.

"Leave me alone," I croaked. "Or you'll be sorry."

"You're the one who'll be sorry," hissed Sharon Downey. I could smell her sour breath. "This is New Girls' Treatment. You can't get away."

Caroline and Jenny were both awake but I hoped neither of them would interfere. They would only get into trouble.

"Leave me alone," I said again. By now I knew exactly where Sharon and Rosalind were standing.

Sharon lunged clumsily towards me and tried to hold my arms down again.

"Submit," ordered Rosalind Hunter. Her hands squirmed under my pillow and grabbed my writing case.

In the playground of my local school, I had

learned how to fight. Also summers of swimming and climbing trees had made me strong. And wrestling with Andrew had taught me a few tricks.

With both feet, I shoved Rosalind in the stomach and she stumbled over backwards.

I heard my writing case clatter on the floor.

At the same moment, I grabbed Sharon Downey by her hair. I could have easily punched her in the mouth and knocked out a couple of teeth but at the last minute I decided not to. Instead I jabbed her upper arm as hard as I could.

Sharon cried out and jumped away from me.

As fast as I could, I slid off my bed, picked up my writing case and stuffed it under my pillow.

At that moment, the door opened and Nurse Blessed stood in the half-light of the landing.

"What's this noise? Sharon. Rosalind. What are you doing out of bed?"

"It's Nancy's fault, Nurse," said Sharon in a choked voice. "She's got something disgusting –"

"I don't want to hear another word from any of you," said Nurse Blessed in a furious voice.

She stomped into the middle of the dormitory and

stood at the end of my bed. Half of her nurse's cap and hatchet face was lit up by the open door. And that half was rigid with fury.

"And as for you, Nancy Cameron, this is the second time I've had to speak to you today."

Her words were like the hiss of a snake.

"Make no mistake, young lady, you watch your step."

"I'm sorry, Nurse," I mumbled hopelessly. "I –

"Silence!"

She stomped back down the dormitory and closed the door hard.

We all heard the clump of her boots as she disappeared down the corridor.

The silence in the dormitory was unbearable.

"You told a lie, Sharon Downey," said Caroline Bigfoot. "You will go to hell."

Sharon snorted unpleasantly. "Shut up, Bigfoot. Or you'll be next."

I sat up in bed.

"If you lay one finger on her, Sharon Downey, I'll punch out your teeth and pull out your stinking hair."

I could barely recognise the hard nasty voice that

was coming out of my mouth. Tears welled up in my eyes. My chest felt like bursting.

On the other side of the room, Sharon Downey slid under her bedclothes.

This time there was no unpleasant snort.

I lay in the dark with my jaws clamped together desperately trying not to cry. I'd been in fights before but never one as vicious as that.

Caroline Bigfoot's mouth touched my ear.

"Don't worry, Nancy," she whispered. "I'll tell Robert everything. He'll know what to do."

Four

A couple of weeks later we were all in the assembly hall for our weekly ballroom dancing lesson with Miss Morelli.

Everyone in House One did ballroom dancing. It was the only way you got to wear white satin dancing shoes with heels. Pumps, they were called in the Official Clothes List. Of course, the heels were barely an inch and we had to wear white socks rather than stockings, but they were heels just the same. And the moment you pulled on your shoes, you pretended you weren't wearing a pleated brown skirt and grey Clydella blouse but the latest ball gown, or in Jenny's case, the shortest, tightest black dress money could buy.

Everyone liked Miss Morelli. She was very tall and very thin with a face that reminded me of a curious pelican. Also she was the nearest thing to exotic that there was at Woodmaston House.

She wore the darkest, reddest lipstick I had ever seen, and her scarlet nails looked long and sharp enough to gut a chipmunk. But the most amazing thing about Miss Morelli was her hair. It was dyed blonde and had the texture of candyfloss. It was rolled up in a huge high stiff cone called a beehive.

We sat on our chairs waiting while Miss Morelli taught Rosalind Hunter how to do the foxtrot.

"Nancy," said Jenny Payne. "Miss Morelli's got a rat in her beehive. I saw it move."

"You saw her beehive move?"

Everyone knew that Miss Morelli's beehive wouldn't move in a hurricane. It was rigid. We were sure that when she got up every morning, she just pushed it back into shape and held it together with more hair spray.

"Not her beehive," said Jenny, kicking me in the shin. "The rat's tail moved." She collapsed into giggles. "It sort of flipped out and wiggled about."

I stared at the whirling golden cone. I couldn't see any rat's tail wiggling about. I knew perfectly well no rat would live anywhere near Miss Morelli's beehive. I had seen rats in the huge smoking garbage dump a few miles up the highway from our house in Quebec. Rats were huge. And they had big yellow teeth.

Nevertheless we'd all heard the story about the woman with the beehive who had complained of headaches.

I shuddered. Suddenly I could see it all. An enormous red-eyed rodent was gnawing a ragged hole in Miss Morelli's brain.

I must have been staring at her in the strangest way, because the next minute Miss Morelli stopped dancing the foxtrot with Rosalind and was standing by my side.

"Ah, dear Nancy," she said in her deep husky voice. Miss Morelli spoke with an Italian accent even though everyone knew she grew up in East Croydon. "You are seeming worried. Come! I teach you ze steps, now."

I stood up and allowed myself to be swung into position in the middle of the room. Rosalind Hunter and I had a special role in Miss Morelli's class. Since I was the tallest in my year and Rosalind was the tallest in her year, Miss Morelli always taught us the men's steps first so that the shorter girls had partners to practise with.

In the beginning, I had been worried about this. I had already decided to be a professional ballroom dancer when I grew up and I knew that my career would never succeed if I could only dance the men's steps. Indeed, I would fail all the Diploma Examinations that were taken at the end of the summer term every year.

But when I mentioned this worry to Miss Morelli, she only grinned at me with her brilliant white tombstone teeth.

"No a problem, dear Nancy," she replied. She lifted me up in her arms so that my feet dangled barely an eighth of an inch above the floor. "We dance like zis."

We swirled and swooped around the room, stepping backwards, forwards and sideways in intricate patterns, and my feet followed hers exactly, swinging like cloth blobs at the end of a rag doll's legs.

"See!" Miss Morelli had cried triumphantly after we finished dancing something I had never learned in the first place. "You vill be a great dancer. You follow ze steps perfectly!"

And so did everyone else.

Miss Morelli had a 100% success rate in all examinations. In fact the only challenge taking the exam was her gin-and-cigarette breath at such close quarters.

However, because this method of dancing was hard on her back, Miss Morelli saved it strictly for examinations. On a week-to-week basis, we kicked and kneed our way through the classic dances, step by step.

A few minutes later, with Miss Morelli's guidance I had the basic back and forth, turn, up and down, turn, back and forth steps of the foxtrot, almost under control.

"Excellent!" cried Miss Morelli, patting my shoulder with her claw-like hand.

She turned to the rest of the class, lolling on their chairs or dancing on their own in different parts of the Hall. "Now vee vill all dance together."

Then she clacked across the room on her high heels to where a gramophone sat on top of a battered grand piano.

"And I vill play you my very new favourite record."

Miss Morelli dug about in her box of EPs and

came up with the same record she played every week.

"Partners, please!"

I turned to look for Jenny but she was dancing with someone else and the next thing I knew Sharon Downey had taken my hand.

"Dance with me?"

"Sure."

And as Russ Conway began to play something tinkly to a foxtrot rhythm, we strode back and forth, up and down the dance floor.

It may seem strange that I should be dancing with Sharon Downey after all that happened that terrible night, especially since Caroline Bigfoot had begged me to have nothing to do with her ever again.

But all that seemed ages ago. Since then everything had changed. Now I felt a secret pride. I had experienced New Girls' Treatment. I was a real Woodmaston Girl.

Also, shortly afterwards, Sharon had started to be really nice to me. And despite Jenny's rolling eyes and Caroline's baleful looks, I was flattered by her attention.

Because Sharon had power.

She knew the lady who delivered the huge metal trays of iced buns at elevenses. So soon I was getting two instead of the usual one. And in the evening when cocoa was poured out, Sharon was in charge of filling up mugs so she could always make sure I was one of the first and my mug was filled up to the top.

In fact there were all kinds of things Sharon could make happen if she wanted.

After a while, I got used to choosing the ideal sized supper because Sharon or someone Sharon knew was serving. So when it was cauliflower cheese, my portion practically dripped over the side. When it was liver and onions, I got lots of potato and a lots of gravy and none of the woolly, tube-filled slabs that other girls had to eat.

And every time Caroline Bigfoot tried to talk to me alone, I pretended I was busy. Then one night after everyone else was asleep, Caroline got up and sat on my bed.

"You can't trust Sharon," she said. She took my hand and held it between her thin cold fingers. "She'll do something bad to you. I know she will."

I looked into her face. It was waxy in the moonlight and her eyes looked huge and worried.

"Don't worry," I whispered. "Sharon can't hurt me anymore. And I'll make sure she doesn't come near you, either."

"It's not me. It's you," said Caroline. "Remember I told you I'd write to my brother?"

I nodded. I'd never known someone as close to their brother as Caroline. She wrote to him every day.

Caroline sighed. "He said the same as me. He said that there are bad boys in his school, too. And you have to stay away from them."

I wriggled my hand free from her grip, although inside I knew I should listen to her. "I'll try and stay out of Sharon's way as much as possible. Okay?"

"Okay."

Caroline slipped back into her bed as silently as a ghost and fell asleep immediately.

Over the following weeks I did try to watch out for Sharon. Caroline was right. In Sharon's world, there was no such thing as generosity. If she did you a favour, it was a debt in the making.

Now as we spun around the assembly hall floor,

Sharon's pudgy hand rested on my shoulder while my arm encircled her football-like waist.

I knew precisely why she had asked me to dance.

"It's my turn for a story tonight, okay?" Sharon spoke wetly in my ear.

"Okay," I said slowly. "But I promised Bigfoot –"

"You're always telling stories for Bigfoot," whined Sharon. "I'm sick of hearing about her stupid brother." She squeezed my shoulder. "You promised me it was my turn tonight "

Her face had a way of going dark and beady if she didn't get what she wanted fast. "I won't give you an extra bun tomorrow."

"I don't want an extra bun. Or more cauliflower cheese."

"I can still make things difficult for you, you know," said Sharon.

I stopped dancing and stared at her. "What is that supposed to mean?"

Sharon's pink face went red. "Nothing," she said quickly. She tried to grin. "I was really looking forward to my story, that's all."

"You'll get one tonight."

"Before Bigfoot," said Sharon quickly.

"Bigfoot's is short this time," I said.

Sharon pulled a face but gave in. "What's it going to be this time? Robert discovers he can breathe underwater?" She laughed meanly.

I shook my head and didn't laugh with her. I'd told so many stories for Caroline about Robert that I almost felt as if I knew him. "I don't know yet," I muttered.

"Well, mine's gotta be about me and Cliff Richard getting married," said Sharon as if she was ordering food at a restaurant. "And this time, it's gotta have a Rolls Royce in it."

Another picture of Sharon's dream wedding floated into my mind.

"How about a big white Rolls Royce all done with ribbons in your favourite colours? Cliff had them dyed specially."

Sharon slumped in my arms. "Oh, Nancy," she croaked. "I want it to be just like that."

"Okay. But first there's Bigfoot, then I've got to finish the bit where Elvis Presley takes Jenny Payne home to meet his mother."

"What about Rosalind? Princess Anne was going to teach her –" Sharon peered at me. "What was it?"

"How to play croquet."

"So what happened?"

"It rained so they watched *The Sound of Music* again."

"Oh yeah. I liked that."

For some reason, Sharon didn't seem to mind listening to Jenny or Rosalind's stories. Although she hated Elvis Presley. His music was rude and his trousers were too tight. Cliff Richard on the other hand was clean and polite, the kind of boy she was sure her mother would approve of.

I once asked Sharon about her family but she didn't seem to like talking about them much. Her mother loved her little sister better than her and her stepfather was always away. I hadn't thought about it before, but maybe that's why she liked my stories so much. She was always the centre of attention.

"So what's Jenny going to do?" asked Sharon, thinking of the night before. "She's wearing city clothes. She's forgotten Elvis is a country boy at heart."

"Exactly."

Sharon stared at me with her piggy eyes.

"Mrs Presley won't like that," she breathed. "You said she was really strict."

It was true. I had said Elvis's mother was really strict and at this moment I had no idea how I was going to get Jenny out of the mess I'd put her into. All I knew was that something would come into my head, just like it did every night when I made up stories to order.

It was Caroline Bigfoot who had started it all. She told me she lived on a farm and one Sunday afternoon when we were all sitting around the rec room waiting for the tea bell, she asked me to guess what her brother Robert liked doing best when he came home in the holidays.

It was one of my dreams to live on a farm. I immediately told her a story about how Robert would start making secret tunnels in the stacks of hay bales as soon as he got home. How he would build a den of his own, hidden right in the middle. How he would have wonderful secret feasts down there. Just like dorm feasts, where you smuggled in sweets and biscuits and hid them under the floor boards. Because a den in a haystack was exactly what I would have wanted, and by the time I finished telling Robert's story, I felt as if I really had one.

"Hey," said Jenny Payne, who had been lounging by one of the two huge silver radiators that ran along one wall. "Can you tell a story like that about me and Elvis Presley?"

She moved nearer and sat down on the arm of the old sofa we were sprawled over.

"It's got to have me winning a singing competition in a fantastic dress." Jenny looked hard into my eyes. "Can you do that?"

In my mind I saw Jenny on the stage. The light from the spotlights bounced off her gold sequinned dress. As Elvis Presley opened the back stage door – he'd heard there was a brilliant new singer performing that night – Jenny was singing better than she had ever sung before. The next thing she knew Elvis was standing beside her. Then he took the microphone into his hands...

"Sure," I said. "I can do that."

Jenny threw back her head and laughed

delightedly. "You and me got a date, doll," she whooped in her terrible Texan drawl.

The tea-bell went.

It was cauliflower cheese, my favourite. Sharon must have heard everything we had said in the rec room, because she put such a great mountain of cauliflower cheese on my plate that creamy yellow sauce poured all over the floor.

"It's my story next," she whispered as I took the dripping plate in my hands.

Five

"She's mine!" wailed Sharon. "I asked her first!"

"So what?" said Jenny with a shrug. "I asked her second." She paused and looked slowly into Sharon's piggy eyes. "And she really likes me."

"But I LOVE her!" wailed Sharon. She pulled a grubby white handkerchief from her pocket and held it up to her face. "She gave me this and she promised to dance with me." Sharon's face went all red and beady. "I bet she didn't give you anything!"

"You'll never know, tubby." Jenny smiled her knowing smile. "She promised to dance with me, too."

"You stay away from Tamsin!" screamed Sharon. Then she promptly burst into tears.

"You're a bitch, Jenny Payne," said Rosalind Hunter as she put her arm around Sharon's heaving shoulders.

Jenny stuck out her tongue. "Takes one to know one."

I buried my face into my copy of *Bunty* and tried

to concentrate on the adventures of the Four Marys. Every week, four girls with the same name got chased to some cliff top. Then you had to get the next issue to read how they shinnied down a rope and got away. It was pretty dumb stuff but it kept me out of the argument that was going on beside me. It was an argument I'd heard time and time again, about an obsession that everyone in the house seemed to have except me and Caroline Bigfoot.

You were nobody unless you had a crush.

When I first heard the word crush, all I could think of was a cold sweet drink full of lots of tiny bits of ice. I used to drink it in Canada. Lemon crush. Grape crush. And lime crush. Lime crush was my favourite because limes were the most exotic and sophisticated fruit I could think of.

But crushes at Woodmaston House were not fizzy drinks with lots of ice in them.

Since I was determined not to repeat the French kissing episode and make a fool of myself, I asked Jenny to fill me in on the details.

A crush was a passion for an older girl. At any rate, having a crush on someone meant you were in love with them. Or you thought you were anyway. The object of your affection was usually in the sixth form. She was always everything you weren't and felt you never would be. Pretty, sophisticated, good at dancing. She was a goddess in human form.

It seemed to me that having a crush was a way of using up the love you felt inside you but couldn't do anything about because you were away from your parents, or your pony or pet hamster.

The obsession with crushes only affected House One. By the time they reached House Two, most girls had dropped crushes, kept ponies, but transferred some of their affection to boys.

Jenny told me that your crush became your reason for living. You dreamed of her night and day. You despaired if she didn't acknowledge you. You went purple if she so much as looked at you in the corridor. And that was before you even got up the nerve to ask her if she would consent to be your crush. Because, as Jenny warned me firmly, before anything could happen, you had to have your crush's permission to fall in love with her.

And some girls, like Tasmin Green for example,

were more popular than others.

This invariably led to problems.

But presuming everything went according to plan and your beloved accepted your adoration, things reached fever pitch on Saturday night. Because that was when the weekly school dance was held in the assembly hall. And your life was not worth living unless your crush agreed to dance with you at some point during that evening.

On dance nights, everyone wore home clothes and only the sixth-formers were in charge. The set up was always the same. Each House had its own circle of chairs arranged along the wall of the assembly hall. Our House circle was opposite the grand piano which was covered in a green baize cloth for the occasion, and piled with 45 rpm records around a boxy red leather record-player.

Since the gramophone was the heart of the evening, the divine beings of the sixth form lounged around it in true pouting Helen Shapiro style.

Sometimes they tapped their high-heeled shoes and stared moodily at nothing. Sometimes, they twisted and jerked to Buddy Holly and "I Guess It

Doesn't Matter Any More." or Bobby Vee crooning his way through "The Night has a Thousand Eyes." But mostly they draped themselves over the grand piano and sifted lazily through the piles of records.

Things were very different for the girls of House One, sitting opposite. Here, eyes stared resolutely at feet, hearts hammered in chests. When, oh when, was the right moment to make the long journey across the hall and ask the vital question: "Will you dance with me?"

To me, the sixth-formers were like the fickle goddesses in one of my favourite films, *Jason and the Argonauts*. In the film, these goddesses sat around on clouds and stirred up trouble in a magical pond. They made horrible things happen to people just to pass the time and even placed bets on whether the poor struggling humans would get crushed, eaten or somehow escape. Sometimes they did helpful things like hand out charmed shields or make oceans dry up.

Like the goddesses, the sixth-formers occasionally took pity on the trembling worshipper who shuffled across the floor towards them. They would rise slowly from their chairs and patiently allow themselves to be clasped about the waist for the length of time it took the Shadows to rumble through "Apache." But other times they would not be so kind. They would lift a bored hand and flick away their worshipper like a pesky fly.

"Go away. I'm busy."

Then they would turn to their drooping companion and laugh meanly behind their hands. If that happened, the worshipper would have to return to her chair knowing that the rest of the House had witnessed her complete humiliation.

All this I learned from Jenny. The strangest thing was that despite the total horror of what she had described, she was sure that if I could just understand how the process worked, I would be sure to find a crush of my own.

But she was wrong. Having crushes on other girls was one of those peculiarly English things that would be forever out of my reach, like junket.

I just didn't get it.

Quite apart from the bizarre girl-worship stuff, the whole process seemed to cause so much trouble.

Why would Jenny want to make things even more

difficult with Sharon by choosing to have a crush on the same girl? So what if Tasmin Green was the prettiest, most sophisticated girl in the sixth form? There must be a couple of others who would do just as well.

Anyway, much as I disliked Sharon's greediness when it came to people and friendships, I thought in this case, she had a fair point. She had asked Tasmin Green first. So why couldn't Jenny choose someone else?

"Because Tasmin's fantastic," Jenny had replied. "Anyway, it's not like falling in love with a boy. It's like –" her voice went dreamy – "it's like they're everything you want to be."

"But you said, you could pass for 16 when you're at home," I said. "Tasmin Green is only a year older than that."

"It doesn't matter how old she is," said Jenny "She's it." Suddenly she got cross. "Anyway, how can you know if you don't even try?"

It was the first time Jenny had ever spoken to me like that. Up until then, I had thought of us like the Three Musketeers, except there were two of us.

Unless you included Caroline Bigfoot, who was a sort of honorary half Musketeer.

"Why should Nancy try if she doesn't want to?" asked Caroline Bigfoot who had been listening to the conversation. "You shouldn't do things you don't understand. Anyway, what's so clever about being unkind? Sixth formers should know better."

Jenny shrugged. "Have it your own way, but I think you're being boring."

I looked at Caroline's serious little girl face. There was something old-fashioned about her. It was as if she would never be part of a world where people wore mini skirts and danced to rock 'n' roll music.

Nevertheless, I didn't like being called boring so to keep Jenny happy and strictly in a spirit of enquiry, I decided to give crushes a try.

The next Saturday night, I dressed in my hippest clothes which were about as hip as an Easter bonnet. I wore a bright red needlecord dress with a needlecord belt and a new pair of flat black patent shoes with black and white clips. The idea was for the clips to match my white socks.

When I paraded my outfit in front of Jenny, she

was combing her fringe so far down over her eyes she could barely see out.

"Great gear, Nance. Uh, real bright."

Jenny, of course, looked as if she had just sauntered off Carnaby Street. She had managed to wangle most of her clothes back from Matron, following the removal of some of the blacker and more glittery bits.

The problem was, I had no idea how to go about this crush thing. What if I made the wrong choice?

"Follow your heart, kid," muttered Jenny, plastering her fringe with water. "It's the only way."

Later that evening I sat in the House One circle, staring across the hall trying to follow my heart.

But my heart wasn't leading me anywhere.

The girls draped over the grand piano just looked liked slightly older girls to me. As for Tasmin Green, she was one of those skinny, monkey clever ones who always made me feel about as dainty as a moose at a garden party.

"Has it worked yet?" said a voice beside me.

Caroline Bigfoot sat down next to me and let her huge sandals swing back and forth under the chair.

I shook my head. "Nope."

"Wanna dance, Nancy?" Jenny's face was bright and excited. She loved dancing and was good at it.

She held out her hands. "Come on! I'll show you how to do the Hitchhiker."

The Hitchhiker was a brand new dance where you wiggled your hips and jerked your thumb as if you were hitching a lift. The idea of it always sent a shiver up my spine. In Canada I was obsessed with magazines with names like *True Murder Stories* or *Crime Monthly*. I knew how every summer hundreds of girl hitchhikers disappeared. And how, in the spring, when the winter snow had melted, their torsos, or other bits of them, were found in shallow graves in woods.

And I always came to the same conclusion. If only they'd listened to their mothers!

"Nancy!" said Jenny impatiently. "The music's gonna start any minute now!"

At that moment Sharon Downey stood up. She was nervous and flushed. She wrung her hands together. They looked like pig's trotters poking out of the cuffs of her lime green tartan dress.

She began to cross the hall.

On the other side of the hall, Tasmin Green picked up a record and looked towards us. A look of annoyance flickered across her sharp, pretty face.

Jenny grabbed my hand. "Do you want to dance or not?"

Somebody shouted "Put on a jive!"

Jenny dropped my hand. Caroline and I watched as she ran across the room. "No," Tasmin was saying to Sharon. "What's the point? You can't jive."

Jenny grinned at Tasmin. Everyone knew Jenny was a brilliant jiver. And the only person who was as good as her was Tasmin Green.

The record needle scratched loudly once. Then Elvis Presley was there. *One for the money! Two for the show! Three to get ready! Now go cat, go!'*

Jenny and Tasmin Green grabbed each other's hands and swung into the centre of the room. Jenny ducked. Tasmin spun. It was as if they'd jived together every Saturday night since they were six.

Sharon dragged herself towards us like a wounded animal.

"I thought you were my friend," she croaked.

I stared into Sharon's face. It was blotchy with rage and hurt and hate all mixed up together.

"You know I love Tasmin," she wailed. "If you'd danced with Jenny, Tasmin would have said yes, I know she would have."

"It's not Nancy's fault, Sharon," said Caroline Bigfoot in a kind voice. "She can't tell Jenny what to do."

"Huh," said Sharon angrily. "She tells everyone else what to do."

"Like how?"

"Like your stupid stories," blurted Sharon. "You think you can play God, that's what you think."

I stared at her puffy face. Last night she had wanted a story about how Cliff gave her little sister a really expensive present for her birthday. It was a Barbie doll with 50 different outfits. By now we all knew that Sharon hated her little sister, but she was her mother's favourite so bribing her was the only way Cliff could get round Sharon's mother to give them permission to go out together.

"Then don't ask for any more stories," I snapped back. "I'm sick of telling them anyway."

Caroline grabbed my hand. "You'll still tell stories about Robert, won't you, Nancy?"

"Yes, yes," I muttered. I couldn't believe it. She looked as if she was going to cry.

"You and your stupid crush," I said furiously at Sharon. "It's nothing to do with me."

The music stopped and Jenny skipped across the floor towards us.

"No hard feelings, Sharon," she said breathlessly. She grinned and patted Sharon's pudgy tartan arm. "Tasmin says she'll dance with you next week."

Sharon grabbed her cardigan from the back of her chair. Tears were streaming down her face.

"I hate you!" she shouted. She turned to me. "I hate both of you."

She ran out of the hall.

"What's bitten her?" said Jenny, flopping down on a chair.

"What did you have to do that for?" I shouted.

"Do what?" asked Jenny, as if she didn't know what I was talking about.

"Dance with Tasmin," I cried. "You've really upset her."

"Why should I let some pudgy dog in the manger stop me doing what I want?" Jenny's voice went hard. "And don't you start bossing me around either." She stood up. "Maybe you're getting too used to that extra bun at break."

"Jenny!" I gasped.

But she was gone, moving easily through a crowd of girls whose names I hardly knew.

I stared at my black patent shoes. Their white and black clips were blurred and wobbly. Bloody stupid crushes. I looked up at the clock. It was almost eight o'clock, which meant the last dance for House One before bedtime.

I couldn't wait to get into bed and be by myself in the darkness.

"Will you dance with me, Nancy?" asked Caroline Bigfoot.

"I'd love to."

We stood in the middle of the Hall and waited.

Someone put on the Everley Brothers.

Whenever I want you, all I have to do is
Dream, dream, dream.

As we swayed and shuffled across the floor,

Caroline rested in my arms as easily as a doll.

"This is Robert's favourite song," she whispered.

It was one of my favourite songs, too. I began to imagine what it would be like to dance with Robert. I'd never danced with a boy before. What if he was really good? I was about as graceful as a baby giraffe.

"Is Robert a good dancer?" I asked.

"He's good at everything," replied Caroline. She laughed. "But I bet he can't do the foxtrot. You could teach him."

"I'd have to meet him first."

As the Everley Brothers' voices swirled and surged around the hall, I began to imagine what it would be like to be friends with a boy like Robert. Somehow I was sure he would be the kind of person who would make everything you did together ten times better.

As Caroline and I slid backwards and forwards over the parquet floor, I tried to imagine Robert's arms around me.

It was easy.

Six

Two weeks later, 50 girls lined up in twos on the gravel in front of House One.

Above us the monkey puzzle tree stretched green and spiky into a bright October sky. We waited in its shadow.

It was Saturday morning, and we were about to set off down town on a shopping trip.

Normally I would have walked down with Jenny but since our last shopping trip, Matron had banned us walking together. Not that she had a real reason. Well, put it this way, she didn't have proof. But she had her suspicions, and they were absolutely accurate.

The last time when Jenny and I had walked together, we had started a rumour that if you wore a certain kind of Eau de Cologne called 4711, the first person to smell it on you would fall hopelessly in love with you.

Or as Jenny put it – make your crush have a crush on you.

Naturally the rumour had ripped through the crocodile line of girls faster than a bushfire.

Everyone knew about 4711. It came in all kinds of sizes. It had a bottle with a turquoise, black and gold label. It smelt nice and strong and it was not expensive. Which meant that if three girls clubbed together and put in part of the two shillings we were allowed each shopping trip, then everyone would be able to afford at least half a dozen shakes from a small bottle. Of course, no one really believed that 4711 had magical powers, but then again, what would happen if it did and you hadn't put any on?

So that afternoon lots of tiny bottles of 4711 arrived back in House One. Just before the dance that night, all the tiny bottles were tipped upside down and rubbed behind ears, onto necks and inside elbows. In the frenzy, quite a lot dripped onto beds, floors and over the furniture.

Sharon Downey had practically rinsed her hair in it. She still hadn't forgiven Jenny for jiving with Tasmin and even the possibility of being able to change Tasmin's mind was enough for her to invest in a whole bottle of her own.

Luckily she never found out it was Jenny and me who had started the rumour.

Anyway, House One stank of 4711 for days and Matron Goring had banned anyone from buying or using it ever again. She had also banned Jenny and me from walking together.

Now Matron Goring was moving up and down the line of girls making her final inspection.

"Coats, hats and gloves," she trilled. She had pinned a round felt hat over her hair and wore a pair of highly polished black brogues and a dark blue wool coat.

"And straight socks, everyone!"

With the instinct of a tracker, Matron Goring turned to where Jenny was already yanking off her garters. Sloppy socks were definitely part of the rebellious look, along with the hoiked up skirt and the pulled down jumper.

"And that means you, Jenny Payne!" said Matron firmly.

Then she pulled out the big silver whistle she wore on a chain around her neck and blew once, hard. "Off we go!"

I was walking with Caroline. That day we were both caught up in our own thoughts and as we made our way down the hill towards the town neither of us spoke much. I knew Caroline was thinking about what she was going to buy Robert for his birthday. While I was trying to work out why Nurse Blessed disliked me so much.

A few days after that awful Saturday night when Sharon had stomped out of the hall, Nurse Blessed had stopped me in the corridor and accused me of looking messy. By the time she had yanked my tie straight, I was rude, deceitful and a troublemaker, and she was putting me in detention on Saturday night.

"You watch out, Nancy Cameron," she'd snarled. "You're so clever that one day you'll cut yourself."

I had no idea what she was talking about, but now I had enough sense to mumble, "Yes, Nurse," and wait to be dismissed.

Besides, since the Tasmin thing, I had tried really hard to keep my distance with Sharon but stay some sort of friends with her at the same time. So I made up stories for her again but I didn't accept the extra buns or bigger helpings she offered. But as with Nurse Blessed, it was impossible to win. If I made up a Cliff story Sharon liked, she complained that hers was shorter than everyone else's. If I refused the piled up plate she pushed towards me, who did I think I was, anyway?

So after a while, I made up stories for me which none of the others knew about.

Now when I lay in the dark, staring at the monkey puzzle tree, I didn't think about Canada, and messing about on the river with Andrew, or taking the dogs for walks along the railway tracks. I pretended I was on Caroline's farm with Robert.

Sometimes we went for picnics by the stream, and afterwards we built a new room on our tree-house. In spring, we looked after stray lambs and fed them with milk bottles. If it was raining, we spent long afternoons in the attic together, because I was sure every farmhouse had a dusty attic full of battered leather trunks. And battered leather trunks were always packed with mysterious letters written on faded crinkly paper. It turned out I was right because one afternoon we even found an old-fashioned

Valentine's day card, with a painting of a lady in a dress made out of real silk.

Even when I made up stories for Caroline, I put myself in the background. Of course, she didn't know that. But if Robert shot past the chequered flag and won the race, while Caroline was there to hand him the champagne bottle, I was waiting in the pits.

The strange thing was that I never felt jealous of Caroline having a brother like Robert. Somehow Caroline was part of a separate world. Despite her big feet, she was made of silvery stuff. Sometimes you felt you could walk right through her.

"Where shall we go?" said Caroline beside me.

I didn't reply. I was building a go-kart with Robert. The problem was, when he'd built one before, he'd always got the steering wrong. But this time we'd get it right because I knew a trick or two about taking corners that would sort things out.

"Nancy?"

"Uh, sorry." I shook Robert out of my mind. "Let's go to the chemist shop first. Then you choose."

Caroline squeezed my hand.

"Okay."

The chemist shop in Moreton-on-Sea was called Hawker & Son. It was my favourite shop. It had a big wooden front with two bay windows, and a heavy glass door with a shiny brass handle. Inside, the floors were wooden and all around the walls were glass-faced cabinets behind tall polished mahogany counters.

Above the cabinets, purple bottles and white china jars sat on high shelves. They had names painted in gold: *Senna, Calcium, Zinc, Magnesium Sulphate*; and, most mysterious to me, *Potassium Permanganate*.

When I went to the chemist, I always followed the same routine. I made my way to the cabinet which held all the surgical tools and bandages. On one shelf there were all kinds of scissors from tiny ones for cutting nails to enormous shears. Then there was a shelf of cut-throat razors which looked like scalpels.

Within seconds, I was a Flying Doctor, zooming down to land in the Australian desert. Maybe my landing was a bit bumpy, but this was an emergency. The morning passed in a blur as I set broken legs, sewed up wounds and saved lives. Then, tired but smiling, I headed back to my trusty little plane with its single prop. In the distance, a small group of people stood and waved. "Thanks, Doctor," they cried. I waved back, swung into the cockpit, and started the engine. Don't thank me. It's all in a day's work.

"You've been staring at those bandages for 15 minutes."

Jenny peered closely at a wide one made of pink crepe. I'd just used it to wrap up the wounded paw of a sheepdog.

"Ugh! They're disgusting! Come on. I've got a really good idea!"

"What?"

"Let's go to the jewellery shop. I've chosen the ring I want Elvis to buy me."

If the chemist shop was my favourite place, Mattons, the jewellers, was Jenny's. Emeralds, amethysts, opals, tourmalines. She knew the names of every single precious stone in the window.

I looked around the chemists. There was no sign of Caroline. "Have you seen Bigfoot?"

Jenny nodded. "She's up the road. She'll meet us

at the jewellery shop."

Five minutes later we were staring into the shop window.

"That's the one I want," said Jenny firmly. She pointed out a ring with an emerald as big as her thumb, surrounded by a crown of diamonds.

That night, I was going to tell Jenny's story first. She wanted one about Elvis arriving with a huge bunch of flowers and a tiny white leather box.

Jenny and I had looked in the jewellery shop loads of times and I knew from what she had told me that emeralds were really expensive. I also knew by then that Jenny's mother was a hairdresser who worked flat-out to send Jenny to school. And her father was a hearse driver.

So the story she had told me on the train about him being picked up by big black car and taken to jail was only half true. The big black car bit was right. Only it was him driving it and he wasn't going to jail. At any rate, there wasn't a lot of spare money around in Jenny's house and the reason she bought her own clothes was because her mother was always working during the day and she didn't have time. So when I made up stories for Jenny, she liked them to be as rich and extravagant as possible.

Now she danced from foot to foot. "Will Elvis buy it, Nance? Does he really, really love me?"

"He adores you, Jenny. He'll do anything to keep you happy."

"Fab!" She pushed me close up to the window. "Now you choose."

I peered through the glass. Unlike Jenny, who had window shopping down to a fine art, I wasn't much good at it. I never got any practice in the Gatineau and, apart from falling briefly and unfortunately in love with our plumber's son, whose name was Ed – he was shorter than me and it turned out he'd only proposed for a dare – I never had a reason to look at engagement rings.

Now as I stared at the rows of glittering jewels one ring caught my eye. It was a single diamond. It was the sort of simple ring I knew Robert would like, too.

As I stared at it, I could feel my face go pink.

With the cunning of a weasel, Jenny knew immediately which ring I was looking at and that I was thinking of someone in particular.

"Who's got a secret?" she chortled, nudging me in the ribs.

I put my face nearer to the glass to hide the blush.

"Sharon's in there," I said. Anything to distract Jenny's attention.

It worked. She stopped looking at me and peered in the window. "Where is she?"

"Looking at bracelets."

"Bracelets!" A mischievous look flitted over Jenny's face. "Let's ask her why Billy Fury would buy her a bracelet."

"It's not Billy Fury," I said, still watching Sharon who now had her back between me and the bracelet stand. "It's Cliff Richard."

"So why should Cliff Richard buy her one?" cried Jenny. "She's got wrists like white puddings." She pulled me towards the door.

"Cut it out," I said.

Jenny stared at me. "What's wrong? I'm only teasing her."

"Exactly. You tease her and I get into trouble." I turned away. "Keep me out of it."

At that moment Sharon walked out of the shop.

"Hey, Sharon," shouted Jenny. "Forget about the bracelet. Nancy says Cliff wants to buy you an engagement ring."

"What are you talking about?" asked Sharon. She sounded confused, and her tongue flicked around her lips.

Jenny's eyes went as big as saucers. "Didn't Nancy tell you," she asked pretending to sound completely bewildered. "It was going to be a surprise but Cliff just couldn't wait."

Sharon looked from one of us to the other. Then her face went dark and beady.

"You think you're so smart," she hissed. "One day, you're going to cut yourself. Both of you."

It was what Nurse Blessed had said to me the other night.

"That is a very nasty thing to say, Sharon Downey," said Jenny in a high singsong voice. "And only a very nasty person would say it." She tugged my arm. "Come on, Nancy. Let's go. There's a funny smell around here."

"You should know," sneered Sharon. "You're

nearest it."

Something snapped inside me. It was exactly what had happened the night Jenny had danced with Tasmin and here I was stuck in the middle again.

"You two make me sick," I shouted. "Stuff your bloody stories!"

I turned and ran down the street.

"Nancy! What's wrong?"

Caroline Bigfoot was standing in front of me.

"You're crying!"

I wiped my nose with my sleeve. "No. I'm not."

"Sharon's done something, hasn't she," said Caroline. "I saw you all outside the the jewellery shop."

"It's not Sharon. It's Jenny. They're always trying to drag me into their fights."

Caroline took my hand. "You should keep away from Sharon, Nancy. She'll make trouble for you. I told you that."

"I don't want anything to do with her," I said in a choked voice. "Why can't she keep away from me?"

"Poor Nancy," said Caroline, gently. She held up a paper bag. "I found something for Robert."

"What is it?"

"See for yourself," she said proudly.

I took the bag and opened it.

Inside was a fishing lure.

"Does Robert like fishing?"

Caroline nodded her head hard. "We've got a little lake on the farm. Last summer Robert went out in the rowboat and caught this really big fish. Only it got away with the hook in its mouth."

I took out the lure. A big hook was tied around with green and orange feathers. Silver tape glittered at the base.

"Don't you think it's a good one?" she asked anxiously. "There were so many. I didn't know which to choose."

I handed her back the lure. "It's perfect," I said. "You need a bit of glitter to catch a fish."

Caroline laughed and carried on walking. "That's what Robert says, too."

That evening when the others rushed off to go dancing, I stood outside the white door of the classroom used as the weekly Detention Room. It was where I had written my first letter home.

While other girls wrote on normal note paper, I had been given a blue aerogramme because my family were in Canada. The postage was included in the aerogramme so I had tried very hard to keep my writing tidy and small so I could fit in lots of news.

I remembered writing the first line. *Dear Mum and Dad and Andrew, How are you? How are the dogs?* It wasn't until I tried to write the next line that I realised how homesick I was. To start with, I didn't know what to say. I almost felt shy, which was pretty weird. But soon I was able to picture my mother and father and Andrew, in the living room of our log house with the seven dogs lying in their favourite places, and I began to write everything I could cram in.

It wasn't that I was unhappy, but coming to school in England was so different from what I'd imagined. It wasn't like the Famous Five one little bit, and I needed my parents to know that. So I wrote my first aerogramme in the same way I sometimes talked with my mother when it was just the two of us in the car. Because talking in cars meant you didn't have to look in someone's eyes when you spoke.

The problem was that on that first Sunday morning, I didn't know that every letter we wrote home had to be shown to the teacher who was sitting with us before we were allowed to seal it. In this case, it was Miss Hutchinson who taught me English and had never once mentioned the subject of my scholarship, or even asked me to write a story for her.

At first, I thought she was only checking the letters for tidiness and spelling mistakes and as I handed over my blue aerogramme, I knew that my letter would have just as many blotches as other girls'. I'd seen them sniffing and rubbing their noses as they wrote just like I had done. And even though I was good at spelling, in the rush to get everything down, I was pretty sure I spelt a few words wrong.

I finished first and stood beside Miss Hutchinson's desk. I couldn't understand why her face got angrier and angrier as she read through my letter. Maybe I'd made more spelling mistakes than I thought. And I had crossed a few things out as well.

Miss Hutchinson turned over the aerogramme and read the last paragraph. Then to my horror, she ripped it in half.

"You are a very selfish girl, Nancy Cameron," said Miss Hutchinson in a furious voice. "How dare you upset your parents? How dare you criticise the school?"

I stared at her. She had a face like a bad-tempered parrot. I had no idea what she was talking about. I hadn't said anything to upset my parents. As for criticising the school, I hadn't done that either, unless telling them how some things were strange was a criticism. Or how Nurse Blessed had called me a liar when I told her I didn't have tonsils.

I could feel tears welling up in my eyes. "But –"

"No buts," said Miss Hutchinson in an icy voice. She dropped the torn aerogramme in the wastepaper basket and handed me a new one.

"I suggest you try again. The extra postage will be charged to your bill."

I walked back down through the rows of girls. Nobody looked up, but as I sat down again at my desk, there was a rustle of paper as everyone scrunched up what they had just written and started again on a clean sheet of paper.

I picked up my pen and stared down at the empty blue aerogramme. This time I didn't feel shy. But my family and our dogs and the log cabin might as well have been on another planet. I had no way of getting through to them.

I knocked on the Detention Room door.

"Come in!" said a young voice.

It was Miss Parkes. I hadn't seen her since the day Sharon had told me Marmite was chocolate sauce.

"Nancy!" cried Miss Parkes. "I've been wanting to see you!"

"Have I done something wrong, Miss?"

Miss Parkes looked at me. "Certainly not. I was wanting to see you to say how sorry I was."

"Sorry for what, Miss?"

"Sorry for not being your teacher." A distracted look passed over her face. "They changed their minds. I mean, the uh, timetables didn't work out." She looked down as if she was embarrassed. "I'm not teaching English at all, as a matter of fact."

"Not even story writing?" I knew immediately that Miss Parkes was very disappointed but she was trying keep it from me because I was a child and she was a grown-up.

"Not even that," said Miss Parkes. She looked into my face. She wasn't hiding her disappointment any more.

"Anyway," she forced herself to smile. "I know I shouldn't be pleased to see you in a Detention Room, but I am. Why are you here?"

"Nurse Blessed said my tie wasn't straight."

"Are you sure that's all?"

I looked into her bright black eyes. She had a pointed chin with a little dimple and short hair that seemed to go every which way.

"Positive."

Miss Parkes shrugged.

"Oh well, never mind."

She picked up a pile of paper and a pencil. "Would you like to write me a story?"

"A story?" I couldn't believe my ears. I was expecting to have to write out lines or copy from a text book. "What about?"

"Anything you like. Although I expect you've written lots of stories for Miss Hutchinson."

I shook my head.

"Not a single one?" asked Miss Parkes. Now she looked really surprised.

I shook my head. "Miss Hutchinson says there's more to English than writing silly stories."

It was exactly what she had said to me when I'd handed her the story I had written especially for the school after I'd won the scholarship.

"Then you shall write your first story for me," said Miss Parkes quickly. She turned away so I wouldn't see the angry look on her face.

I took the pile of paper from her hands. "Will anyone else read it?"

"Do you want them to?"

"No."

"Then I won't show it to anyone."

I decided to write a fairy tale. You can make up all kinds of different monsters in fairy tales.

I picked up the pen. *Once upon a time* – Nurse Blessed's hatchet face floated into front of me – *there was a cruel, disgusting monster. She was made half of flesh and half of iron...*

Seven

It was Jenny who decided we needed a psychiatrist.

"Either that or a hypnotist," she said firmly. "You can't have a Beauty Parlour without one or the other."

Sharon was sitting in her pyjamas on her bed, hemming a handkerchief for our needlework class. "What's a psychiatrist?" she asked slowly.

"Someone who listens to someone else's problems," said Jenny. "So when you get your toenails painted, you get to, you know..." She shrugged. "Sort things out."

"Like you and Jenny sorted things out after you made Nancy cry at the jewellery shop," said Caroline Bigfoot.

"Oh," muttered Sharon to her feet.

"Exactly right," said Jenny gaily.

Jenny and Sharon had made a truce. They had both agreed that they couldn't live without their stories, so the evening I was in Detention, Jenny went up to Sharon at the dance and said she was sorry. To make things completely better, she said her crush on

Tasmin Green was over, and that she would never dance with her ever again, unless she asked Sharon's permission first.

Which led to Jenny and Sharon dancing together for the first time, which in everyone's view cemented the Deal.

Now it was Sunday morning, a week after the Deal. Sunday was the only morning we didn't have to strip our beds before breakfast and make them again after. That gave us an extra 15 minutes and we had lots to talk about. For the first time ever, our dormitory felt like a real team.

A few days ago, Matron Goring had called a special House meeting to tell us all that the Headmistress wanted each dormitory to think of ways to raise money for the school's new library.

At the time, people came up with ideas like selling raffle tickets or doing Bob a Job, like the Boy Scouts. But I thought all that sounded a bit boring.

It seemed to me that running a Beauty Parlour for the morning fitted the bill exactly. Everyone was obsessed with their appearance. Once we'd got the necessary information from Jenny – since her mother

had a hair salon, it was decided she was the one to ask
– I was sure we could raise lots of money for the
library.

At first Matron had been a bit unsure. She was
worried about things like scissors and red nail
varnish. But these problems were easily overcome.
Under no circumstances would we be allowed to
have such things in our possession.

Instead, for manicures and pedicures, we were to
be allowed only emery boards, clear nail varnish,
orange sticks and buffing pads. For up-to-the minute
facial treatments, we could have a big tub of cold
cream. For the hair styling, as much water and as
many hair clips as we could find.

As for face make-up, there wouldn't be any.

Where perfume was concerned, after much
persuasion from Caroline, who we knew was our
most persuasive spokesman, Matron agreed to let
bygones be bygones and that a dab, but only a dab,
of 4711 could be applied to the satisfied customer at
the end of her treatment.

So it was that both sides went away from the
negotiations smiling.

Which was why on this Sunday morning there were a lot of plans to be made. It was our last chance to make a list of what we needed for our Beauty Parlour before we all went away for half term.

Jenny had been delighted to take over as Official in charge of getting supplies. For the first time, she felt really proud of her inside knowledge of beauty treatments and hair salons. In fact, now that everyone knew that her mother was a hairdresser, I had immediately put Mrs Payne in charge of Elvis' glossy quiff. Which was a real vote of confidence since Elvis was extremely fussy about his hairstyle.

Jenny propped herself up on her bed and picked up her pen and exercise book.

"Okay," she said firmly. "This is what we need."

"Nancy will be the psychiatrist," interrupted Sharon.

"I am not going to be a psychiatrist," I said from where I was stuffing clothes into my chest of drawers by the window. "That was never part of the plan." I turned. "And don't forget it was my plan."

"Okay, okay, Nance," said Jenny quickly. "Let's forget about psychiatrists." She opened the notebook.

"We want our Beauty Parlour to be really good, don't we?"

Everyone nodded.

Jenny picked up her pen. "Who knows how to spell peroxide?"

From the start, we all agreed there was no point having a beauty parlour if it wasn't the real thing. So we had to get all kinds of exciting stuff together, and that did not mean one tub of cold cream and a bottle of clear nail varnish.

As for the ban on make-up, Jenny rolled her eyes. Matron just didn't know anything about the outside world. It would be crazy to let her ignorance wreck our Beauty Parlour.

Besides, when the moment came and Matron saw how much money we made, she would see everything our way. It was obvious. What else could happen?

Jenny called out item after item as her pen scratched over the page. Foundation, preferably deep beige or sun-kissed orange, lipstick, eyeliner, eye shadow, mascara, eyebrow pencil –

"What's an eyebrow pencil?" asked Sharon.

"It's for drawing in eyebrows," explained Jenny writing down the words "False Eyelashes."

"But I've already got eyebrows," said Sharon.

"Tweezers," replied Jenny.

Sharon looked puzzled and went back to picking her feet.

"Everyone will come," said Caroline Bigfoot in an excited voice. "'Specially since the big party's that night."

The timing of our Beauty Parlour was my particular stroke of genius. It was to be held on Saturday afternoon before the United Nations Party, which was the biggest event in the school's social calendar.

The United Nations Party was supposed to be a celebration of the international character of Woodmaston House. Every year there was a special ceremony, where one girl from every country represented in the school stood in a circle, held a lighted candle and called out the name of her country.

Since I was the only Canadian in the school, I had been given the honour of representing Canada. So along with Mahti, who was representing Persia and was the only girl I knew who could vomit at will, we had practised standing in a circle and calling out our country's name.

Apart from me being told off for not knowing the difference between "calling out" and "shouting", everything had gone smoothly.

One of the other reasons the United Nations Party was so special was because it was the only occasion we were allowed to wear the "One Party Dress" that was on the Official Clothes list. Since almost every girl in the House would want to look her best, we were pretty sure our Beauty Parlour would not be short of customers.

Jenny looked up from her list and fixed me with a business-like eye. "Now, about this psychiatrist problem –"

"Don't be crazy, Jenny," I said. "Apart from the fact that I'm not doing it, I've never heard of a Beauty Parlour with its own psychiatrist."

"Trends are changing, Nance," said Jenny in a serious voice. She stabbed her finger at the page. "Kids get worried before parties. They get attacks of pre-party nerves."

"Oh, shut up, Jenny," I muttered.

"I've never worn make-up before," said Sharon breathlessly. "Can you get it off with soap?"

"Of course, you can," said Jenny "Now hair dye, that's different."

"I'd never dye my hair," said Sharon in a shocked voice.

"Quite right, too," said Jenny smoothly. "Your hair looks lovely as it is."

Sharon went pink and picked at her feet.

"See, Nance," said Jenny, sounding pleased with herself. "Keeping the customer happy, that's the one."

"You'd make a wonderful psychiatrist, Nancy," said Caroline Bigfoot. "You always say nice things."

For the first time, I wished Caroline Bigfoot would stuff her sandal where her mouth was.

"Excellent," said Jenny. "Nancy will be in charge of saying nice things."

At that moment, the dormitory door opened and Nurse Blessed stamped in. "Why aren't you dressed yet?" she snapped. "The breakfast bell is in five minutes."

"We've been talking about our Beauty Parlour, Nurse," said Caroline Bigfoot as she poked her skinny arms into a long white vest. She looked proudly at me. "Please, Nurse. Nancy's going to make everyone happy, just like my brother does."

I wished the floor could swallow me up.

"What nonsense are you up to now, Nancy Cameron?" snarled Nurse Blessed. For some reason, her voice sounded particularly dangerous.

"It's not nonsense, Nurse," said Caroline calmly. She pulled her huge school dress over her head. "It's for our Beauty Parlour. You should be proud of us."

The whole dormitory froze.

No one spoke to Nurse Blessed like that.

We waited for the explosion. But nothing happened.

Instead, as Nurse Blessed stared at Caroline Bigfoot, an odd expression flickered across her face. It was anger, but something else as well. Something unsure. I looked away so she wouldn't see that I'd noticed. But I didn't look away fast enough.

"Get dressed, Caroline," said Nurse Blessed. "And as for you," she gave me a look of pure poison, "Stop meddling!"

The door shut with a bang.

Jenny turned to Caroline. "If I'd said that, she'd have dragged me out of the room." She swung off her bed and stuffed her exercise book under the mattress. "Stupid old bitch."

No more school books! No more French!
No more sitting on the old school bench!
No more spiders in my tea, making googly
eyes at me!

It was half term. We whooped and yelled all the way to Victoria Station.

On the train, a few of us felt for a piece of paper that Jenny, as Head of Supplies, had given out the night before.

I pulled mine out and looked at it.

I didn't even know what false eyelashes looked like.

Later that morning, I sat beside my grandmother in the front seat on the top of the bus as it rattled past Hendon Central and along the High Street. Just for a little while, we had run out of things to say.

It was the first time I'd seen her since the beginning of term and while I told her lots about my new
school, I decided to leave out bits like Nurse Blessed
and New Girls' Treatment. Instead, I'd told her all
about my friends and the United Nations Party and
the Beauty Parlour we were going to open. I saved my
best piece of news to the very last. That Caroline
Bigfoot had asked me home to her farm on the last
Visiting Sunday before the end of term.

"That'll be nice, dear," replied my grandmother,
who didn't have a lot of time for farms. "Has she any
brothers and sisters?

"Just one brother," I said and quickly looked out
the window so she wouldn't see my face go pink.
"His name's Robert. He'll be there, too."

But my grandmother appeared not to be listening.

"And have you written any stories yet?"

I knew she wanted to hear that I'd written lots
and lots, and that the teachers were very pleased
with them. But I also knew that I couldn't tell her
the truth. Because my grandmother was feeling a bit
anxious about things since six weeks into the term,
the Headmistress had written to my parents and

given them her Assessment Report of my abilities. Unfortunately she had mixed me up with another girl who could barely read or write. A copy of the Assessment had been sent to my grandmother.

My grandmother had been devastated. She thought that I'd broken my promise to work hard. That week she sent back every letter I'd written from the beginning of term with their spelling mistakes underlined. Lucky for me, a couple of weeks later, when the Headmistress had written to my parents suggesting special coaching to improve my basic language skills, my parents had made a rare and frantic telephone call and the mistake had been discovered.

Now, staring down on the busy pavements of Hendon High Street, I didn't want to upset my grandmother again.

"I'm writing a fairy tale," I said.

"What does your teacher say?" asked my grandmother, sounding pleased.

I remembered Miss Parkes' face a couple of days after my detention. She had made a special visit to House One to make sure I was all right.

Eight

"Wow!" cried Jenny. "Where did these come from?"

"My grandmother got them," I said proudly.

Despite all the odds, my grandmother had come up trumps. She liked clothes and jewellery and while she only wore lipstick, the idea of a Beauty Parlour was almost like a dressing-up box to her. So she understood immediately that a good Beauty Parlour had to have lots of different things to try on.

So the day before I came back to school, we had taken the bus to Oxford Circus and spent the morning in Hamley's looking at dolls' house furniture, although this time we didn't buy anything. Then in the afternoon we went to the cosmetic counter of Selfridges and she bought half a dozen boxes of false eyelashes. Some of them were even studded with tiny rhinestones.

It wasn't just me who had come back with "the goods", as Jenny described them.

Sharon had done particularly well. She had raided her mother's make-up draw and taken half a dozen brand new lipsticks and four brand new bottles of scarlet and purple, cherry and shocking-pink nail varnish. The only thing she had forgotten was the Remover Liquid, but we all agreed that this didn't matter at all.

Rosalind had been in charge of eye make-up because she had two older sisters and had come back with stacks of hardly used pencils, paints, brushes and shadows in every colour imaginable.

As for Jenny herself, dressed up as a 16 year-old, she had managed to buy several bottles of permanent blonde and permanent black hair dye.

Finally Caroline Bigfoot had come back with several different shades of face make-up, and a giant-sized bottle of fake tan that Jenny had added to her list at the last minute.

We sat on the dormitory floor and stared excitedly at our pile of bottles, boxes and creams.

The Beauty Parlour was in business!

Jenny let her head flop over the sink while I gently rubbed her head. Her thick straight hair was heavy and soft with conditioner.

"Too much conditioner, Nance," she said. "But you've got the hang of the massage."

Over the past few days, Jenny had been teaching me everything she knew about Beauty Parlours. Now as I gently rubbed her base of her head – it makes 'em relax, Jenny said – her eyes flicked open.

"You'll never believe this," she whispered.

"What?"

"Promise you won't tell anyone."

"Promise."

"You know all that brand new stuff Sharon brought back?"

"Yeah. Her mother must have been furious."

I poured warm water over her hair and rinsed out the softener. I squeezed out her hair with a towel.

"I don't think her mother had all of that new stuff. I think Sharon nicked 'em from a shop."

The towel was cold and damp in my hands.

"You're joking."

"Nope," said Jenny. "Besides where would she get the money from?" She pulled the towel off her head. "By the way, never leave a wet towel on a customer's head. It makes their brains go soft."

Twenty minutes later, I knew all about eyeliner, eye shadow, mascara and eye pencil. I knew the order in which they went on and how to apply them with a steady hand. I knew how to pluck eyebrows and how to paint lips. And last but not least, I knew how to get a completely natural-looking tan from a bottle. "Easy," Jenny had said. "You rub on lots and lots, wait for a couple of hours and say you've just come back from Spain."

I laughed but I was feeling edgy. I couldn't believe Sharon was a thief.

On the morning of the United Nations Party, we got up early and transformed our dormitory into the Beauty Parlour that Matron was expecting.

One iron bed was left in the middle to act as a make-up couch. Beside it was a trolley with the one big jar of cold cream.

Two chairs sat on either side of a small table with emery boards, orange sticks, a bottle of clear nail varnish and a small buffing pad.

On the wash basin, a bowl of hair clips sat beside a huge pile of fresh towels.

Sure enough, Matron was delighted.

"I'm very proud of you, girls," she said. "And so is the Headmistress." She gave us a shining smile. "I might even pay you a visit myself, now that everyone is going to look so fresh and pretty."

The door closed behind her.

"Fresh and pretty," muttered Jenny as she bent down to prise up a floorboard and dig out our store of bottles and creams. "What a load of crap."

Caroline Bigfoot sat behind a chest of drawers that had been turned into a reception desk. In front of her was an exercise book which had "Appointments" written across the front in big, black writing. It was completely full.

Beside her Rosalind poured out orange drink into lots of plastic mugs. At the last minute, Matron had given us permission to serve squash and biscuits during treatments and Rosalind had volunteered to be our Beauty Parlour Waitress.

Rosalind had rounded up almost every mug in the house because word of our wider-than-advertised range of services had secretly spread. And since most girls had never worn make-up, let alone lots of make-up, almost everyone wanted to give it a try.

The only thing nobody wanted to try was a change of hair colour.

At first Jenny had been disappointed, but now she was philosophical. "I'll put out the bottles any-way," she muttered. "Maybe someone having the full makeover will change her mind."

There were only half a dozen girls having the full makeover and since Jenny and I were the two beauti-cians, we had drawn straws to decide who got who.

I had drawn Sharon.

"At least you didn't get Scabby Josephine," said Jenny. "Or Barbara Greentooth."

Josephine Murley looked weird because her face was covered with red blotches but Barbara Powers was one of the strangest girls I had ever met. Her teeth were green because she never brushed them and she never washed if she could possibly avoid it. Matron had to practically frogmarch Barbara to the bathroom when it was her bath night. And since we had bath nights every second day and were not allowed more than six inches of water, it was hardly likely that her skin would get worn off. As for the clothes, Barbara never changed hers. On Saturday mornings Matron made a special trip to Barbara's dormitory and emptied her chest of drawers onto the floor where they went straight into the laundry bag.

So to begin with no one could understand why Barbara had put her name down for a complete makeover.

No one that is, except Sharon. Because it was the same reason Sharon had put herself down.

Barbara had a crush on the ugliest girl with the greasiest hair in the sixth form. Her name was Edwina Tottle and Barbara adored her.

Now that Jenny was out of the way, Sharon had been dreaming of her dance with Tasmin Green at the United Nations Party for weeks.

So it happened that after lunch, Mahti stood guard in the corridor outside to warn us if Matron was coming and the Beauty Parlour opened its doors to customers.

Hours later, I'd plucked more eyebrows, painted more lids, and rubbed more goo on more faces than I could ever have thought possible. Even girls who didn't want the full makeover, which included fake tan and hair-colouring, wanted to try a little make-up. So the idea was that the ones who had gone for the really adventurous look (orange tinted skin, the purple and blue eye shadow and the extraordinary long eyelashes) would be able to lie low until the bell went. Then they would mingle in the crowd, run past Matron with their heads down, and make a mad dash to the assembly hall.

Luckily for us, it was Nurse Blessed's day off.

As the afternoon wore on, a succession of happy, richly-coloured customers passed through our door and the pile of coins in our tin sandwich box grew larger and larger.

Sharon was my last customer. By now I was getting fed up with washing hair and painting faces and my back was sore from standing. I also had things of my own I wanted to think about. Tomorrow I was going out with Caroline Bigfoot, and Robert would be there. And it was his birthday.

Every time I thought about it, I felt fizzy inside. Not just because I wanted to meet him more than anything else but because I'd decided to give him my lucky squirrel's foot for a birthday present. It was the most precious thing I had and I knew he'd like it. Also I hoped it would make him think of me when he looked at it.

Caroline already had the whole day planned out.

"We'll have a picnic then we'll play on the lake in the rowboat," she said.

I thought she was teasing.

"In December?"

"Why not?" Caroline hugged herself. "It's Robert's favourite thing to do and it's mine, too." She grinned at me. "Anyway, you can make a fire so we can keep warm."

"Won't your parents mind?"

Caroline shook her head. "They'll come with us. They like picnics, too."

Of course, Jenny who had been listening in and watching my face like a hawk put two and two together immediately. "Tell you, what, Nance," she said. "Before you go, I'll do your hair for you." She punched my arm. "It can only make you more irresistible."

Now as I stood, rubbing shampoo into Sharon's

red stringy hair, all I could think of was the next morning and the moment I met Robert.

"I've got a present for Tasmin," murmured Sharon.

"That's nice."

I scraped up a handful of lather and plopped it into the warm soapy water.

"I'm going to ask her to think of me whenever she wears it," sighed Sharon.

Maybe because I'd thought the same thing about Robert and my squirrel's foot or maybe because Sharon had stolen the make-up, suddenly touching her made me feel sick.

I reached for a bottle of conditioner and forced myself to rub the sides of her head.

Sharon squirmed in her chair and pouted. "I thought you were supposed to say nice things. You haven't even asked me what my present is."

"What's your present?" I moved my hands to the base of her head and kneaded her skull with my thumbs.

Sharon closed her eyes.

"It's a bracelet."

I reached for the jug of water to rinse her hair.

"Oh, don't stop," pleaded Sharon. "Please. Just once more."

There was something about the way Sharon squirmed. It felt horrible, as if I had a revolting slug between my hands. I tried to stop a shudder going through me.

Sharon opened her eyes.

"You think I'm ugly, don't you?"

"Of course I don't."

"Then why did you stop?"

I tipped some more of the softener into my hands and massaged the sides of her head again.

"Sorry. I guess I'm getting tired." I forced myself to smile at her. "Uh, what does your bracelet look like?"

"It's real gold with a little sea horse charm."

"Where did you get it?"

"From the jewellery shop in town," murmured Sharon. She looked straight at me. "I had to have it because of Tasmin."

My hands stopped moving. I saw Sharon standing by the bracelet stand. Then I saw her coming out of the shop. She'd looked edgy and nervous and her tongue was flicking over her lips.

I guess I would never have worked it out if Jenny hadn't told me about the lipsticks and the nail varnish. Suddenly I was absolutely certain that Sharon had stolen the bracelet she was giving to Tamsin.

"Why have you stopped again?" whined Sharon.

"Conditioner," said Jenny beside me.

I looked down at Sharon's lumpy face. If anyone ever found out about it, she would be expelled.

Sharon's eyes flicked open. "What's wrong?"

"Nothing."

"Then hurry up. I don't want to be here all day."

"Conditioner," said Jenny again.

I picked it up and gave it to her.

Jenny stared at the bottle then she stared at me.

I'd been rubbing cream peroxide into different parts of Sharon's hair for over 20 minutes.

Nine

Forty girls stood on the landing in their party dresses. Their faces were tinted orange or plastered with thick pancake make-up. Their eyes were the colour of bruised blueberries. Some of their lips were bright enough to stop traffic.

A few girls had a two-tone look. They were the ones who had been caught in the bathroom trying to rub it off before being dragged to the first floor.

Everyone looked pretty peculiar.

But the girl whose appearance was nothing short of exceptional was Sharon. She had bright pink lips, turquoise eye shadow, deep beige skin and a glittering false eyelash which drooped down over her right eye.

But it was her hair that made her look truly spectacular. Jenny's attempts to dull down the yellow of the peroxide with black dye had turned Sharon into something that looked like a crazed hyena pup.

She stood sobbing hysterically and clutching Matron's hand.

As for Matron herself, for the first time ever, her

face had lost all traces of pretty red squirrel. Her lips were pressed together and her cheeks were quivering with rage.

"Who is responsible for this?" she demanded in a low furious voice.

"It was Nancy," squealed Sharon. She rubbed at her chestnut-coloured cheeks. "She did it."

"It wasn't just Nancy," said Jenny. "I bought the dye."

"And I bought the brown stuff," said Caroline Bigfoot in a stout voice.

"What brown stuff?" said Matron.

"The brown stuff that's on Sharon's face," replied Caroline Bigfoot.

"Step forward, Dürer."

Jenny, Caroline, Rosalind and I stepped forward and waited.

"I trusted you. Especially you, Nancy," said Matron in an icy voice. "We agreed rules for your Beauty Parlour and you promised to keep to those rules."

She turned to me.

"What have you got to say for yourself?"

"I'm sorry, Matron," I muttered. "I didn't mean to put dye on Sharon's hair. I thought it was conditioner."

"No, you didn't," snarled Sharon. "You did it on purpose."

"Be quiet, Sharon," snapped Matron. "I was not talking about your hair. I was talking about keeping promises."

"Please, Matron." Caroline Bigfoot's face was shining. It was as if she wasn't going to let anything or anybody wreck our achievement. "We only wanted our Beauty Parlour to make lots of money for the library."

She held out the sandwich tin she'd been hiding.

"Three pounds, four shillings and seven pence," she said proudly.

She looked into Matron's face with her wide, serious eyes. "No one would have come if we didn't have real make-up, Matron."

This was the moment when we knew Matron would suddenly see things our way. And everything, except a few dirty towels, would go back to normal.

"That's not the point, Caroline," snapped Matron angrily. "You disobeyed my rules and you lied to me."

She turned to Rosalind who was looking slightly sheepish with one blue eye and pink lipstick hastily smeared from her lips on to her cheek.

"Did you know about this, Rosalind?"

"Yes, Matron." A confused looked passed over Rosalind's face.

"Is there something you want to say?" asked Matron.

Rosalind stared at her feet. "Jenny was right, Matron," she whispered. "It wasn't just Nancy's idea. We all helped. I'm sorry, Matron."

I tried to catch Rosalind's eye but she didn't want to look at me. I knew she didn't like me much, but I realised then that she didn't like Sharon much either.

Matron turned to Sharon.

"What have you got to say for yourself, Sharon?"

"They didn't tell me anything, Matron."

"So why did you let them put make-up on your face when you knew perfectly well I had forbidden it?"

Sharon's face screwed into a tight ball.

"I'm waiting for an answer, Sharon."

"Because I wanted to look pretty at the party," she muttered.

She pulled at her hair.

To my horror some of it came out in her hands. "Now everyone will laugh at me." She glared at me with her red-rimmed, hyena pup eyes. "I hate you, Nancy!"

"Stop it, Sharon," ordered Matron. "No one will laugh at you because no one from Dürer is going to the party this evening."

Shock rippled through the landing.

All the other girls looked at us with a mixture of pity and embarrassment.

Suddenly we were lepers.

"You will return to your dormitory and go straight to bed," said Matron.

Rosalind rubbed her fist across her face. Caroline didn't appear to mind at all and Jenny just shrugged. It occurred to me that we might all get a bit hungry if we were sent to bed now. But I stared at my hands and said nothing.

Sharon lifted her tear-stained face. "Can't I go?" she croaked.

"Absolutely not," said Matron.

Sharon stepped backwards as if she had

been slapped.

"But I didn't do anything," she sobbed. "I didn't do anything. Ask Nurse."

"Be quiet Sharon," snapped Matron Goring. "I will not listen to another word." She looked up. "The rest of House One, wash your faces and –"

But before she could finish speaking, Sharon turned and ran down the corridor, howling at the top of her voice.

"Please, Matron," said Caroline Bigfoot. "Nancy didn't mean to dye Sharon's hair. It was an accident."

"Don't believe a word of it, Matron!"

Nurse Blessed stomped into the middle of the landing. "That girl is lying."

Caroline Bigfoot's face went as still as a pond. "I'm not lying, Nurse," she said.

Nurse Blessed moved a step closer to Caroline. She was so angry, she looked as if she was going to explode.

"Don't you talk back to me, young lady," she snarled.

Matron stepped up beside Caroline almost as if to protect her. "Nurse!" Her voice was sharp and quick.

"The matter has been dealt with and I consider it closed."

The two adults glared at each other. Unspoken words cracked like sparks in the air.

I stared. I couldn't help it. Something was going on between them that I had never noticed before.

"Canada!" I shouted out as loud as I could.

I was dressed in my school uniform and standing in a circle of girls wearing party dresses and holding candles. I was supposed to feel humiliated because everyone else was wearing party dresses but I didn't feel humiliated. All I wanted was to get out of there and go back to my friends as soon as possible.

Fifteen minutes earlier, Matron had summoned me from the dormitory. I was told to dress and take my place for the ceremony. There was a record number of countries represented in the school and the Headmistress had specifically demanded I had to be there to keep the record in place.

The atmosphere in the dormitory was terrible. Matron had cut most of Sharon's hair off so at least she didn't look like a hyena pup any more. But even though I tried a couple of times to apologise, she refused to speak and looked right through me.

"Let her stew in her own juice," said Jenny in a flat voice. She turned over in her bed. "She's a rat and she knows it."

"I'll report you if you talk like that," muttered Rosalind, but the fight had gone out of her voice.

"Oh, shut up, Rosalind," said Jenny. She glared at Sharon. "As least you're not a liar, like some people."

It was still light.

Sharon sat on her bed and glared back.

"I don't see why you're so cross, Sharon," said Caroline Bigfoot. "All you've had is a haircut. It's Nancy that's in the most trouble."

"Sharon's missing her dance with Tasmin," sneered Jenny. "Only she doesn't know that Tasmin wasn't going to dance with her anyway. Because Tasmin thinks Sharon is weird and ugly and pathetic."

At that point Matron had opened the door and told me to get up and put on my uniform.

Now I was running back down the corridor with a huge lump of special party cake wrapped in a napkin and stuffed under my jersey.

I'd stolen as much as I could because we were all hungry and I wanted to give everyone a piece. Even Rosalind and Sharon.

I ran past the changing rooms with their smell of mud and old boots, then slowed down as I came to the corridor where our dinner overalls were hanging.

At this point, I had a choice.

I could either take the main front stairs up to the landing, or I could go round the back way, up towards the bathrooms, which meant I would have to go past the surgery and Nurse Blessed might be in there. But the way past the surgery was nearer the dormitory and the sooner I got rid of my bundle of cake, the better.

I decided to go round the back way.

The back stairs were small and twisty with no bannister. If you ran up quickly enough, they hardly creaked at all.

I ran up the stairs and past the surgery.

I was a step from my dormitory door when I felt a hand grab my shoulder and twist me round.

"Thief," hissed Nurse Blessed. "You're coming with me."

My mind froze. How could she know about the

cake under my sweater? As she frogmarched me down the corridor, all I could think was how to get rid of it fast.

Nurse Blessed pushed me through the door into the sanatorium.

"I'm locking you in, Nancy Cameron," she said in a voice like a ragged razor blade. "Get undressed and get into bed."

Then she slammed the door behind me and a bolt shot into place.

I stared around me. I was in a room that was more like a prison than a san. It stank of disinfectant and there were bars on the windows. Someone had thrown my pyjamas and dressing gown on a bed in the corner.

I wanted to turn and bang on the door. There must be some mistake. Where was Matron? But I knew Nurse Blessed would be back any minute and if they found me with the cake then whatever was going to happen would be ten times worse.

My mind kept coming back to the same question. How could Nurse Blessed have known I had stolen the cake? Had she seen me taking it from the food table at the party?

She couldn't have. The room was empty. Everyone else was at the party.

Anyway, there was no time to think about that now. I had to get rid of the cake. I could either dump it down the loo or throw it out the window.

If I dumped it down the loo, would it float?

Yes.

Somehow I had to get it out of the window.

I reached in under the bars and tried to shove up the window. It was stuck. The catch at the top was shut and looked as if it hadn't been opened since it was last painted.

I needed something to knock it loose. On the other side of the room, there were some books piled up on a bedside table. I grabbed one and used it to hit the catch. It was enough to unstick it.

As fast as I could, I eased up the window. It made a terrible squeaking noise, but there was nothing I could do about that. Then I unrolled the crumbly parcel from my sweater and dropped it over the sill.

Someone turned the bolt in the door.

I pulled the window down, stood in a far corner

and shook the crumbs from my sweater. Then I jumped back over to the bed where my pyjamas were lying.

Matron came in.

My first thought when I saw her was relief. Even if she did know about the cake, no school was allowed to lock a girl up. Anyway, I could tell her the truth. I'd stolen the cake because everyone was hungry. It wasn't right to send girls to bed with no supper.

I opened my mouth to explain everything to her. Then I took one look at her and shut it again.

Matron's face was made of stone.

She reached into her pocket and pulled out a bracelet with a sea horse charm dangling from it.

I thought I was going to be sick.

"Have you ever seen this before, Nancy?" said Matron, slowly.

As I shook my head, Nurse Blessed walked into the room.

It was true. I'd hadn't seen it. But Sharon had told me about it. I felt my cheeks going pink.

"You're lying," snapped Nurse Blessed.

"I'm afraid this is serious, Nancy," said Matron. "Very serious indeed."

I stared at her.

So that was why Nurse Blessed had called me a thief.

I could hardly choke out the words. "You don't, you don't think I stole it?"

Matron looked steadily into my face.

"Rosalind found the bracelet under your pillow."

She laid it over her hand. "A bracelet just like this was stolen from Mattons a month ago." She folded the bracelet in her hand. "Sharon saw you in the shop."

The chill in my stomach turned hard as ice.

"Have you got anything to say for yourself?" asked Matron

I tried to force myself to think. Whatever I said now would be remembered and if I got it wrong, they would hold it against me. I had to get things straight in my head.

Sharon must have put the bracelet under my pillow while I was at the party. If she couldn't give the bracelet to Tasmin, what better way of getting revenge than planting it on me?

But where were Jenny and Caroline? They must have see her hiding the bracelet. Why hadn't they stopped her? And what about Rosalind? Had she seen what Sharon was doing and decided to keep her mouth shut? Or had Sharon somehow forced her to keep silent?

"Nancy?" repeated Matron. "Did you hear me?"

If she had spoken, I hadn't heard a word she said.

"Have you got anything to say for yourself? I will be taking you to the Headmistress tomorrow."

"But I'm going home with Caroline Bigfoot tomorrow," I blurted.

"You are not going home with anybody, Nancy," said Matron Goring. "You will almost certainly be expelled."

"Expelled?" I gasped.

"Stealing is a crime," said Matron. "We don't want girls who steal in Woodmaston House."

"But I didn't steal it!" I cried. Suddenly my knees were trembling and my head felt hot and dizzy.

"Then who did?" asked Matron.

I forced myself to look straight into her face. "I

think Sharon stole the bracelet, Matron. Jenny was with me. I never went inside the jewellery shop."

"You little liar."

Nurse Blessed took a step towards me. "Sharon Downey is a decent girl."

"Nurse!" said Matron sharply.

She turned to me. "How do you know Sharon stole the bracelet, Nancy?"

"Because I saw her through the jewellery shop window," I said. "Jenny was with me. She'll tell you."

"Why didn't you report this at the time?" asked Matron Goring.

"I couldn't Matron," I croaked. "I wasn't sure."

Matron Goring's eyes narrowed. "What do you mean you weren't sure?"

"It was when I was washing Sharon's hair, she told me about the bracelet."

"Did she tell you she stole it?"

I shook my head miserably. "But I saw her in the jewellery shop and –"

Before I could stop them, tears began to roll down my face.

"You must believe me, Matron."

"Get into bed, Nancy," said Matron Goring. Her face was set. "You will stay here until we see the Headmistress tomorrow."

She didn't believe me. And if Matron didn't believe me, why would the Headmistress?

The thought of getting expelled for something I hadn't done made me feel physically sick. I knew my parents and my grandmother would believe me. Apart from anything else, the school had already got things wrong. But this was different. No matter what my family believed, if I was expelled, all my friends would think I was a thief.

Jenny was my only hope.

"Please, Matron," I croaked. "Ask Jenny. She was with me. She'll tell you."

Matron Goring held my eyes.

"Jenny Payne has run away from school," she said. "The police are looking for her now."

I felt as if I'd been punched.

Ten

At last, Robert and I were on our own. From the moment we met it was as if we had known each other for years. And I was right about the squirrel's foot. It was the perfect present. He loved it.

We sat side by side in front of the fire beside the lake. It was me who suggested roasting marshmallows. I had a bag of them from Canada and Robert had never roasted marshmallows before.

I picked out a green one.

"This is frog flavour," I told him. "And frog tastes of chicken. I read that in a book."

Robert picked a yellow one. "This one's canary flavour and canaries taste of custard." He grinned at me. "I made that up."

He speared the marshmallow with his stick and picked up a white one. "This one tastes of polar bear."

"Polar bear's my favourite."

I could feel the shape of him sitting on the grass beside me and shifted closer. I'd never been so happy in all my life.

There's a trick to roasting a marshmallow. If you hold it in the fire too long, the stick burns and breaks and then the whole lot falls off. So since the lake was nearby we soaked our sticks in water. That way the stick doesn't get too hot, and as long as you keep turning it, you should end up with a perfectly roasted marshmallow.

The first time Robert tried, he burnt the end off his stick. The second time, he got it just right, but burnt his mouth because he didn't wait for the marshmallow to cool down.

"That's why I stopped making toffee," I told him. "I can't even look at that stuff without feeling it burn."

Robert laughed. "You're always imagining things, aren't you? My sister says you make up amazing stories for everyone."

He twirled a perfectly roasted marshmallow in the air and sucked it into his mouth.

"Would you make up a story about me?"

I stared at him. He looked a bit like Caroline, but not so serious. His eyes were lighter green with dark lashes and his hair wasn't curly like Caroline said, it was thick and wavy.

I forgot to watch my marshmallow and it dropped in a long white gloop.

There was no way I could tell him that I had already made up hundreds of stories about him for his sister. He might think it was weird or really pathetic. But I didn't want there to be any secrets between us. I wanted Robert to know everything about me so we could understand each other and trust each other. Then I was sure nothing could go wrong.

"Sometimes I get tired of making up stories," I said. I chucked my stick in the fire and picked up a new one. "But if you stop, people get mad at you."

Robert tapped my knee with his finger.

"Come on, Nancy. What can Sharon do to you if you don't marry her off to Billy Fury?"

"It's Cliff Richard," I muttered.

Robert rolled his eyes. "Who cares if it's Cliff Richard or Guy the Gorilla?"

"That's the problem, Robert."

I began to talk in a rush.

"You see, everyone does care. It's all they ever talk about. Sharon really wants to believe she's going to marry Cliff Richard. Last night, I was telling her a story about how Cliff had to order an even bigger wedding tent because he'd sent out so many invitations and she suddenly got really mad at me."

"What do you mean, mad at you?"

"She started to shout at me." I tried to imitate Sharon's angry, hysterical voice "Cliff didn't ask my parents, did he? Because they can't come. I hate them."

I jabbed my stick in the ground. "She said I'd ruined everything and then she started to cry."

"You ruined everything?" Robert pulled a face. "Come on, Nancy, you're exaggerating."

"No, I'm not!" I tried to keep the hurt out of my voice. Why didn't he believe me?

Robert shrugged.

"Then stop telling stories."

"I tried that and then it was even worse. They said I was making them unhappy on purpose."

"Seems to me you lose either way." He picked up my stick and put a marshmallow on the end. "Anyway, why are we talking about nutters like Sharon when we've got lots of stuff we want to do ourselves?"

"Because Sharon has blamed something terrible on me," I whispered. "And I'm going to get expelled." Before I could stop it, tears began to fall down my cheek.

"Nancy!" Robert moved beside me and and put his arm around my shoulder.

I held my breath to stop myself crying.

But it didn't work. I sobbed and sobbed.

"Be quiet, you little thief! You'll wake the house with your blubbering."

There was a flick of a switch and the room turned white and hard.

I opened my eyes and blinked. For a moment, I couldn't think where I was. Then I remembered the voice and I knew the dark, blurred face against the bright ceiling light belonged to Nurse Blessed.

"The sooner you are expelled from this school, the better," said Nurse Blessed.

"But Nurse. I didn't steal the bracelet."

I struggled to sit up. I heard my voice but I didn't know how it had got there. It was somewhere between a croak and whisper.

"Why do you hate me so much? What have I done to you?"

Nurse Blessed was standing a few feet from my bed. She moved nearer to me and suddenly I was aware that the door was closed and we were alone.

"You're a bad influence and you're a trouble-maker," snarled Nurse Blessed. She practically spat at me. "And you tell filthy, disgusting stories."

I felt as if she had chucked a bucket of ice over my head.

Nurse Blessed's ogre face was so close to mine I could smell her breath. It was hot and foul.

She grabbed my wrist. "Men kissing young girls. Men touching their bodies." She dropped her voice to a low, harsh whisper. "You're a dirty little slut."

Her words crashed around my head. Yet I knew exactly who had told her those lies.

Sharon.

But why?

I tried to pull my wrist away but Nurse Blessed wouldn't let go.

"Please Nurse, if Sharon –"

Nurse Blessed exploded with fury.

"How dare you mention Sharon Downey's name?" she shouted. Her eyes stabbed into mine like two knives. "I won't hear another word from your filthy mouth." Her fingers tightened around my wrist.

Suddenly I was terrified. She could suffocate me. No one would know.

I opened my mouth to scream.

"Shut up!"

Nurse Blessed clamped her hand over my lips.

My mind sprang apart. I sunk my teeth into her hand and bit down as hard as I could.

Nurse Blessed lurched backwards and pressed her hand against her chest. Blood seeped over her starched white uniform.

"You little devil!"

I jumped out of bed and ran across the room. As I pulled at the door, I felt her hands grabbing my pyjamas.

"No! No! No!" I screamed at the top of my voice.

The door flew open and Miss Parkes was standing there.

I threw myself at her.

"Help me!" I sobbed. "Help me!"

Then I slipped down through her arms and fell onto the floor.

I woke up with a jolt.

It was dark except for a watery silver light that shimmered behind the curtains. I almost cried out with relief. I wasn't in the san. There were blinds in the san.

Something was scratching and tapping at the window.

For a crazy moment, I thought it was Jenny. She'd come back. She found a ladder somewhere. She was climbing up to me.

I sat up and jerked back the curtains as far as they would go.

Thin white clouds whizzed past a three quarters moon. It was a windy night. As I watched, a branch from the monkey puzzle tree scratched and tapped against the window.

I was in a small room and there was an empty bed beside me. On the far wall was a big painted chest of drawers. On the wall above it was a picture of a bunch of sunflowers.

As soon as I saw the sunflowers, I knew I was in a two-bed dormitory called Van Gogh at the top of House One.

Someone must have carried me up three flights of stairs.

I tried to remember what had happened after I fainted in Miss Parkes' arms but I couldn't. Instead my mind filled up with nightmares. Matron's stony face. The dangling bracelet. The feel of Nurse Blessed's hand clamped over my mouth.

I curled up into a ball to stop myself from crying.

As I grabbed the sheets around my head a furry lump tumbled onto my shoulder. It was my stuffed monkey. Someone must have brought him up to me.

If someone cared enough to bring me my monkey, then maybe they cared enough to help me out of the trouble I was in. I pressed my face into the monkey's brown velvet head and made myself think.

Now I knew there were two charges against me. I was a thief and I told disgusting stories. And as long as Jenny was gone I couldn't prove I hadn't been in the jewellery shop, so it was Sharon's word against mine.

In fact it was Sharon's word against mine over just about everything.

There was only person left who might be able to help me and that was Miss Parkes.

The question was, could I be absolutely sure she was on my side?

She must have had a reason for standing outside the door of the san. The more I thought about it, the more I was sure that Miss Parkes had known that I was inside. But how could she have found out? And how long had she been standing there?

I tried to remember the exact moment I pulled open the door handle. Had the door been shut or, if it had been open, could Miss Parkes have heard everything?

Again I felt Nurse Blessed's fingers grabbing at my pyjamas. I felt my hand pulling at the door...

The door had been open.

Miss Parkes could have heard every word. That would mean Nurse Blessed could never deny what happened.

For the first time I felt a flicker of hope and tears dribbled down my face. It was Nurse Blessed who should be expelled from the school, not me. She belonged in prison for what she had done. I held my monkey against my chest and squeezed him hard.

I was sure it was Miss Parkes who had left him with me. It was her secret message. She was on my side. I wasn't to worry any more. I wasn't to cry any more. Everything would be sorted out.

The door opened.

Caroline Bigfoot stood there in a huge white night dress. "You're coming home with me, tomorrow, Nancy," she said. "I don't care what anyone says."

I stared at her.

"Do they still think I stole the bracelet?" I whispered.

Caroline nodded.

I put both hands over my face and tried to stop myself screaming.

Nothing had been sorted out at all.

Caroline sat beside me and began to rock back and forth.

"This is all Sharon's fault," she cried. "I knew she would do something bad. Right at the beginning, I told you. I told you."

"For chrissakes, Caroline," I muttered. "You're not making any sense. What good is that going to do me now?"

Caroline stared straight through me.

"You should have listened to Robert and me."

A gust of wind moaned outside the house. The monkey puzzle branch tapped harder at the window. I looked at her face. It was waxy like a candle. Two red spots appeared on her cheeks.

I took her hand. "Caroline. Are you all right?"

Caroline's eyes were huge. "I'm all alone, Nancy," she cried. "No one's in the dormitory but me and Rosalind. And Rosalind cries all the time."

I felt myself slipping towards the edge of a cliff.

"Isn't Jenny back yet?"

Caroline shook her head.

Then she held out her arms. "Hug me, Nancy. I only feel safe with you."

It was what she'd said on the playing fields the first time we met.

Again I saw her waxy face and huge eyes. I pulled her towards me. She was as floppy as a knitted doll.

We sat like that for a few minutes. As each minute passed, Caroline held on to me tighter and tighter. The sunflowers in the picture had turned silver in the moonlight. I had no idea what time it was but there were still lights on behind a couple of windows in the street, so maybe it was around midnight.

I was sure now that Caroline would be the last person I saw before Matron took me to the Headmistress.

"Caroline."

"Mmm." She nuzzled her face closer to my shoulder.

"Can you tell me what happened last night? I've got to know before tomorrow morning."

"When we found out you'd been shut in the san, Jenny said she was going to run away. She said she wasn't staying in a place run by psychos any more. When I came back from the loo, she was gone."

I saw myself in the san. I was staring at the bracelet in Matron's hands, asking myself how Sharon could have hidden it under my pillow without Jenny and Caroline seeing her.

Now I knew and my heart sank like a rock in a pond.

Caroline's breathing turned into a long shuddering wail. "Oh Nancy! I'm so sorry! It's all my fault! If only I'd been there, I could have stopped Jenny from running away!"

I sat Caroline up and held her away from me. Her eyes were full of tears.

"It's not your fault, Caroline," I said. "But you've got to help me. You've got to try and remember everything. Did anything happen much later on, after I'd been locked up in the san?"

Caroline sniffed and wiped her eyes with the sleeve of her night dress.

"Will you hold me again?" She snuggled back up to my shoulder. "Someone started banging on Matron's door. We all woke up because it was so loud. Then I heard Miss Parkes' voice and she sounded really angry. I got up and looked through the crack in the door."

Caroline rubbed her hand across her face as if she didn't know how to tell me what she saw.

"I thought you were dead, Nancy," she sobbed.

"Miss Parkes was carrying you in her arms and you were all white. I thought you were dead."

I held her in my arms but I couldn't speak.

"I heard Miss Parkes say words like 'disgusting' and 'criminal'. Then I saw Matron and Miss Parkes carry you up the stairs." She smoothed the hair away from my forehead. "That's how I knew where to bring your monkey."

"You brought him up?"

Caroline nodded. "But you were so asleep I didn't wake you. Anyway, when I told Sharon and Rosalind what I'd seen through the door, Rosalind said if Sharon didn't own up, she'd tell Matron herself."

"Tell Matron what?" My voice was barely a croak.

"That she saw Sharon put the bracelet under your pillow."

My head went all fizzy. I didn't understand.

"Then why does everyone still think it was me who stole the bracelet?"

"Because Sharon called Rosalind a liar and said she wouldn't own up to something she didn't do."

I could barely speak. "Hasn't Rosalind told Matron?"

Caroline shook her head. "Matron isn't here. Miss Hutchinson is in charge. There's no point Rosalind telling her. She doesn't know anything."

I nodded miserably. "When's Matron back?"

"I don't know, but Rosalind says she'll tell her as soon as she comes back." Caroline pulled at my sleeve. "Don't forget Miss Parkes, Nancy. She must know the truth, too."

"How would she know if Matron doesn't even know?" I asked angrily. "Anyway, where's Sharon? If she tries to stop Rosalind, I'll punch her teeth in."

"Sharon's shut in the san," said Caroline. "Nurse Blessed put her there because she scratched Rosalind's eye when Rosalind told her to own up."

Caroline shifted on the bed and her face caught the moonlight coming in through the window. For the first time, I noticed there were enormous dark circles under her eyes. She must have been awake for most of the night. Suddenly I felt completely worn out.

"What's the matter, Nancy?" asked Caroline. "You're looking at me in a funny way."

"I'm tired," I said. "And you are, too."

Caroline squeezed my hand. "You're right. We'll

go to sleep now." She sounded almost happy. "We've got a busy day tomorrow."

I tried to smile at her but said nothing.

Caroline picked up my monkey where he'd fallen onto the floor. "Don't let him get cold," she whispered. Then she turned and walked quickly out of the room.

I lay back on my bed. My body felt heavy as lead. Then I fell asleep as if I was falling into space. I dreamt I had a bracelet locked around my wrist like a handcuff. A tiny figure of Sharon dangled from the chain.

Eleven

Dawn was a huge strip of red. The wind had dropped and only a few stars sparkled in an inky blue sky. I pulled down the window and stared across the road. The air was cold and clear. In front of me the monkey puzzle tree stood absolutely still. Beyond it, across the street, big pointed brick houses sat silent behind high dark hedges. On the top floor of each house, the curtains were pulled behind the small window that was set under the eaves.

I stood in front of the identical window in an identical pointed brick house. I was wearing a brown woollen dress I found folded up in the chest of drawers. It stank of mothballs but it just about fitted. In another drawer, I found a pair of socks, a vest and some old-fashioned baggy pants. There was even a pair of heavy lace-up shoes.

I was glad I'd found the clothes. Wearing pyjamas was like wearing prison uniform.

Now I was waiting for the last star to disappear. I'd given myself till then before I opened the door and walked down the three flights of stairs to Matron's room. If Matron wasn't there, I'd go to House Two and look for Miss Parkes. I didn't care any more what trouble I got into. Now I knew the truth, I wasn't waiting any longer.

I stared into the dark street and thought about Jenny. It must have been scary for her on her own at night. I tried to imagine how she felt as she turned out of the front gate and walked away from the school. Or maybe she ran, keeping near to the hedge so no one would see her. I wondered whether she'd tried to make her way home. But how could she? Even if she got to the station without being stopped, she had no money.

Beyond the branches of the monkey puzzle tree, one pale star still hung in the sky. I took a deep breath and was about to open the door when a car engine rattled outside the house. Tyres crunched on the gravel. I stepped quickly back to the window.

I was sure it was Jenny and I wanted to be the first to tell her what I knew. I wanted to hang my head over the sill and yell, just so I could see her face looking up at me.

I pulled up the window and stuck out my head. Two headlight beams swung across the front of the house. The car stopped.

I opened my mouth to yell.

Nurse Blessed stepped into the light of the headlamps. She was wearing a dark overcoat. A round black hat was pulled down over her head. Her black boots clattered over the gravel as she crossed in front of the car and set down a large suitcase.

A tall straight-backed woman stepped into the light. It was the Headmistress.

"Nurse Blessed, I deeply regret your departure but I had no choice. You were employed by the school as a bona fide nurse and your granddaughter was granted a place on that basis."

The Headmistress's deep voice carried easily in the still air. I stood with my hands in the window sill unable to move. What on earth was going on? I could understand that Nurse Blessed was leaving the school but why was the Headmistress talking about a granddaughter? Nurse Blessed didn't have a granddaughter.

As if in slow motion I watched Nurse Blessed

open the boot of the car and heave in the suitcase. Then she motioned with her hand towards someone I couldn't see.

My stomach turned over.

Sharon stepped out from under the porch. She was holding a small overnight case. Underneath her school overcoat she had on home clothes. The light from the porch shone on her face. It was blank and frozen. She walked towards the car as if she was walking in her sleep.

I couldn't bear to look at her. As I turned away and stared into the dark spiky branches of the monkey puzzle tree, two faces floated in front of me. The same bullet head. The same cold, piggy eyes. They even had the same squat, rolling walk.

Suddenly I understood. When I fell out with Sharon at the very beginning, I had fallen out with her grandmother, too. And the times when Nurse Blessed left me alone had been the times when Sharon wanted me to be her friend.

"Sharon."

It was Matron's voice. It sounded kind.

I jerked my head round and stared down again.

I saw Matron walk up to Sharon. She bent down and put her hands on Sharon's shoulders. It was something I'd seen her do so many times.

"Don't touch her," snapped Nurse Blessed. "You've done enough harm already."

I could sense Matron wanted to speak but the Headmistress held up her hand for silence. Matron straightened up and stepped backwards.

Nurse Blessed opened the car door to let Sharon get in. Then she turned to where Matron and the Headmistress stood in the porch light.

"God rot you both," she said. Then she spat on the ground and climbed into the car.

As the car drove away, the last star disappeared.

The Headmistress's voice cut through the night. "Thank you, Matron Goring. I'm deeply sorry for the distress this has caused you."

"I would never have known had it not been for Eleanor Parkes," replied Matron. Her voice sounded worn out and empty. "I must take full responsibility for –"

"Matron Goring," said the Headmistress, firmly. "The discovery that Nurse Blessed falsified her qualifications left me with no choice but to order her immediate dismissal. I take full responsibility for the matter."

Their footsteps crunched over the gravel.

"As you say, Headmistress," said Matron. "I only hope that Nancy Cameron -"

"Nancy Cameron is a spirited girl," interrupted the Headmistress. "She will recover. Now if you will excuse me, I think we could all benefit from some sleep."

Matron stood head bowed. I watched the Headmistress turn and walk away.

The light in the front porch went off. I heard steps coming up towards the landing.

I pulled open the door and ran down the stairs.

Matron was standing by herself on the landing.

When she turned towards me, her face was so tired and white, it looked as if it had been bleached. Tears trickled down her cheeks.

She opened her arms and I ran into them. She rocked me back and forth as we stood wrapped around each other.

"Oh, Nancy," she whispered. "I'm so sorry. I'm so

terribly sorry." She held my face in her hands. "Can you forget all the terrible things that have happened?"

I couldn't speak and when I tried to nod, my head only hung down further over my chest. All I wanted was the feel of her arms around me.

"There's someone who's been waiting to see you for a long time," said Matron. "For most of the night as a matter of fact."

She took my hand and led me across the landing towards her private sitting room.

I stopped before she could open the door. There was something I had to ask her.

"Matron?"

"Yes, Nancy."

"Is Caroline ill?"

Matron gave me a puzzled look. "No. Is something the matter?"

I told her the truth. I couldn't bear any more lies and I was sure Caroline wouldn't get into trouble for coming up to see me. There'd been too much trouble for that to count any more.

"She came to see me in the night," I said. "She told me everything Rosalind said." I swallowed. Despite myself, I couldn't meet Matron eyes. "You know, uh, about the bracelet, and uh, Sharon."

"I know, Nancy, I know," said Matron, gently.

"Thing is, Matron... She looked really ill. She had black bags under her eyes and weird red spots on her cheeks. And, and, she said things that didn't make any sense at all."

"Caroline is very tired," said Matron. She paused. "And she's very worried about you and about Jenny."

"Do you think I should tell her –"

Matron shook her head.

"I don't think we should wake her, Nancy, if that's what you mean. There'll be time enough later. And she needs her sleep."

Matron smiled and ruffled my hair. "Especially since you're both going out today."

It was an odd smile. I was sure Matron was hiding something from me.

"Do you promise Caroline's not ill, Matron?"

"Caroline's not ill, Nancy," said Matron, slowly. "But she needs her rest."

She opened the door of her sitting room. Jenny Payne stood in front of us. She blinked and rubbed her face. She looked as if she had just woken up even though she was wearing a short black dress with purple stockings.

"Nancy! Nancy!"

Jenny's face split into a huge grin and she threw her arms around around my neck. "Are you all right? Are you all right?"

"Shh!" whispered Matron, gently. "You'll wake up the whole house."

I looked into Jenny's face. Her eyes were smudged with black eyeliner but her long, thick false eyelashes were still in place. She looked like a raccoon with two tame spiders resting on its eyelids.

For the first time in ages, I wanted to burst out laughing.

Matron looked at us both and smiled. This time it was a real smile. "So here you are again, you two," she said. "Sit yourselves down and I'll go and make you breakfast."

Jenny tapped the top of her second boiled egg with a spoon and picked off bits of the shell.

I whacked mine off with a knife and dipped in a

toast soldier.

At first when we had tried to talk, we both got so choked up, all we could do was cry. So we'd try again, only a few words at a time and still we couldn't finish what we wanted to say.

Then Matron had arrived carrying a tray covered with tea and toast, boiled eggs, two kinds of jam and a bowl of hot soapy water and a washcloth for Jenny.

There was no hurry, she said. We could take as much time as we liked.

It must have been the soapy water and the washcloth that had fixed it. Jenny wiped her face clean and we began to eat. By our second egg we felt better.

"You know something, Nance?" said Jenny. Her face was thoughtful.

"What?"

"I don't think I look 16 at all. When Miss Parkes saw me in the street, she knew exactly who I was." She bit into her own soldier. "Funny thing though. You'd have thought she'd be cross, but she wasn't. And she didn't bring me back here either. We went straight to her room."

I thought about what the Headmistress and Matron said to each other after Nurse Blessed and Sharon drove away. When I'd told Jenny, she didn't seem at all surprised.

"Do you think it was Miss Parkes who found out Nurse Blessed wasn't a real nurse?"

"Almost positive," replied Jenny. "Because when I told her you'd been locked in the san by the old bitch, she shot out of her room like a bullet."

I shuddered. What if Jenny hadn't run away? What if Miss Parkes hadn't stopped her? "Thank God you told her."

"Damn right, I did," said Jenny. "I told her everything, but at first I wasn't sure."

"What do you mean?"

Jenny chewed on her toast. "At first I didn't know whether I could trust her. Okay, she wasn't cross when she found me but how could I know whether she was on our side? I mean, she kept asking me questions."

"What sort of questions?"

"Mostly about Nurse Blessed and you," said Jenny. She looked at me. "She seemed to have a pretty good idea the old bag was giving you a hard time."

I told her about the fairy story I'd written in detention.

"Did it star a monstrous ogre in a nurses's uniform?"

"Something like that. She even came to see me afterwards to make sure I was all right."

"Yeah, well," said Jenny. "Whatever it was, I decided I could trust her, so I told her everything. Your stories about Elvis, Cliff and Robert. Even about Rosalind and Princess Anne. Then I told her about seeing Sharon in the jewellery shop." Jenny looked up at me. "Strange thing, though."

"What?"

"It was your stories she was interested in most. Especially Bigfoot's ones." Jenny grinned. "I thought she'd go for Elvis Presley myself."

She tapped the top of a third egg. "And ever since you told me all your stuff, I've been trying to work things out."

I stared at her. "What do you think?"

"I think as soon as Miss Parkes carried you out of the san, she made Matron go straight to the

Headmistress. Remember Bigfoot heard her saying something was "criminal"? I think Miss Parkes threatened to call the police if the Headmistress didn't get rid of Nurse Blessed right away."

I put the empty eggshell top back on the empty egg. It was a perfect fit. "Otherwise why would they leave so quickly?"

"Exactly," said Jenny. "And Sharon had to go, too, because she was going to get expelled anyway."

I shrugged. "You couldn't tell anything from her face."

"I don't give a damn about Sharon," said Jenny. She shoved her spoon into her egg so the yolk poured over the edge. "Oh, by the way, Miss Parkes wants to see you this morning." She pulled a face. "Sorry, she asked me specially to tell you and I forgot."

My insides started shrinking. "Why this morning?"

"I dunno. Something about Bigfoot."

"Bigfoot?"

I thought about Matron's odd smile.

"I think Bigfoot's ill."

"What do you mean 'ill'?"

I told her about the red spots on her cheeks and

the way she talked that didn't make any sense. "Matron said she was just overtired."

Jenny thought for a moment.

"I think Matron's right, Nance," she said. "I mean, you know how serious Bigfoot is. She was really upset when we heard about you." She bit her lip. "So was I."

Neither of us could look at each other again. We picked our tea cups and slurped noisily.

"Jenny?"

"What?"

"Why do you think Sharon told those lies about my stories? That was almost the worst bit."

"I think she hated you for being able to make them up," said Jenny.

I rubbed my hand across my forehead. "Do you think that's why Nurse Blessed picked on me all the time?"

"Yup," said Jenny in a matter of fact voice. "After all, you weren't any worse than me and she didn't go for me like a bloody rhino."

"But I still don't see why Sharon had to tell Nurse Blessed my stories were disgusting." I could feel my throat tighten.

"Don't you understand, Nance? " said Jenny. "It was the only way Sharon could use your stories to destroy you."

Suddenly the room felt completely empty, as if there was no furniture and the walls were painted white.

I looked at Jenny "Will you tell Bigfoot everything's all right?"

"Of course, I will," said Jenny quickly. "Now go and see Miss Parkes before it's too late."

Five minutes later, I scrawled a note on a piece of a paper and shoved it under Miss Parkes' door.

Dear Miss Parkes,

I tried to see you but you weren't there. Thank you for all the things you've done to help me.

Yours truly,

Nancy Cameron

P.S. I'm going out with Caroline Swithins today but I will try to see you when I come back.

*

"Nancy!" Caroline grabbed my hand and dragged me towards a boy who was mending a bicycle. "This is my brother, Robert."

The boy stood up. He had thick wavy hair and green eyes. I stared at him. I was sure I'd met him before.

He stared back. He was thinking the same thing.

"Robert," said Caroline. "This is Nancy. She comes from Canada."

Neither of us spoke.

Caroline turned and laughed at me. It sounded like the jingling of a toy bell at Christmas. "Aren't you going to say hello?"

"Hi," I said.

"Hello," said Robert at the same time.

I blushed and and tried not to look at my feet.

Robert grinned. He'd gone a bit pink, too. He wiped his hand on his overalls and held it out.

"Caroline's told me lots about you."

I shook his hand. I was glad it was sticky with oil because maybe then he wouldn't notice that mine was sweaty and hot.

"Nancy likes climbing trees," announced

Caroline.

"Fantastic," said Robert. "We've got a great tree in the orchard."

"And it's got a treehouse," said Caroline, proudly. "Mum says we can have tea there if we want to."

I grinned like an ape because I couldn't think of anything to say. I'd been looking forward to meeting Robert for so long. Now I was acting like a tongue-tied idiot in a brown woolly dress.

"Stay cool, Nance," whispered Jenny in my ear. "He's only a boy."

She laughed a low throaty laugh. "Mind you, if there's more where he comes from, I'm telling Elvis to mind his manners."

"Shut up, Jenny," I whispered. "He'll hear you."

"'Course he won't," whispered Jenny. "He's too busy looking at you."

"What do you think?" asked Jenny.

"What?" I mumbled.

"For gawd's sake, Nance," said Jenny, pretending to be cross. "Here am I taking up my precious time making you look pretty and you don't even know

I'm here."

"Sorry."

My eyes slowly focused on the blur.

I was sitting in a chair in front of my chest of drawers staring into a mirror. Caroline was running back and forth in front of the bay window peering onto the road. Jenny stood behind me with a comb in her hands.

"Well," said Jenny. "Do you like it? It's sort of Diana Dors meets Elizabeth Taylor."

I stared at myself in the mirror. The same square face. The same slightly upturned nose. The same curly hair. Except that now bits of it were flat.

"I think you look lovely," cried Caroline Bigfoot in a high squeaky voice. She laughed and danced from foot to foot. "Lovely. Lovely. Lovely."

I'd never seen Caroline so happy and excited. Apparently she'd hardly listened when Jenny told her everything that had happened. It was as if it didn't matter any more. Sharon was bad. Now she was gone. That was that.

Even when I tried to talk to her myself, all she did was put her hands over her ears and waggle her head from side to side.

"No more nasty things, Nancy," she cried. "We're happy now. No more nasty things!"

It was different with Rosalind. Jenny told me that when she woke up, she couldn't see out of the eye Sharon had scratched and she was really upset. So Jenny had hardly any time to talk to her before the doctor arrived and took her to hospital.

"I did the best I could, Nance," said Jenny. "But she kept crying and saying how sorry she was. Even when I told her it was all right now and nothing was her fault."

Poor Rosalind. I wished I could have seen her before she left. I understood now that she'd been bullied by Sharon just as much as the rest of us.

"They'll be here soon!" cried Caroline Bigfoot. She climbed on a chair so she could see over the hedge and down the road. "I know they will! They'll be here soon!"

Jenny was watching me so I made myself turn my head from side to side to admire her hard work. I knew perfectly well it would blow back to frizz in five minutes. "Thanks, Jenny. It looks very nice."

"That's okay. You look really, really pretty." She punched me lightly on the arm. "There's just one thing."

"What?"

"You stink of mothballs."

Two hours later, I was sitting beside Caroline's mother on a deep saggy sofa in a hotel in Eastbourne. I was trying really hard to hide my disappointment. We didn't go home to their farm and we didn't pick up Robert on the way. We drove straight to Eastbourne and nobody even mentioned that there had been a change of plans.

Mrs Swithins turned and smiled at me.

"Caroline's so fond of you, Nancy," she said. "I almost feel as if I know you myself."

Through the huge window opposite us we could see Caroline playing with her father along the sea front. He was holding her left hand as she tiptoed along the sea wall. She waved her right hand up and down as if she was pretending to fall.

I watched Caroline clamber into her father's arms

and wrap her arms around his neck. It was as if she'd turned back into a little girl.

Mrs Swithins sipped at a gin and tonic. "We wanted to thank you for being such a good friend."

There was something tight in her voice. It sounded as if what she was saying was difficult for her.

Mrs Swithins reached out and took my hand. "I know it's been hard for you."

I was hot and dizzy again. What was she talking about? She couldn't know anything about the stolen bracelet or Nurse Blessed. But somehow I knew it was something else. Maybe Caroline was ill after all, and Matron hadn't wanted to tell me. Maybe she thought that after everything that had happened, I wouldn't be able to cope.

I began to gabble.

"Caroline's told me so much about you," I said. I could hear my voice sound high and edgy. "I've always wanted to live on a farm. And I'd love to have a lake and catch fish."

Mrs Swithins' hand jerked in her lap.

"My brother and I have a river near us. But we don't have a rowboat." I laughed nervously. "Mum says it's too dangerous. Anyway, Caroline told me Robert was teaching her to row. I'd love to learn to row. Caroline said Robert might teach me one day." I felt my face go pink. "Caroline's always telling me about Robert. They must –"

Mrs Swithins' hand tightened around mine.

I looked up. To my total horror, I saw she was crying.

I thought of Caroline's hollow eyes. Her white face. The red spots on her cheeks.

"What's wrong, Mrs Swithins? Is it Caroline? Is she ill?" Tears welled up in my eyes. "Last night, she seemed so strange. I asked Matron –"

My throat shut tight and I couldn't talk. And I couldn't look at Mrs Swithin's face either. It was too unbearably sad.

"Caroline is ill, Nancy," whispered Mrs Swithins. "But she's ill in a different way."

Tears rolled down her face.

"Oh, Nancy," she cried, suddenly. Her voice broke. "We were sure Caroline would have told you. She was so close to you. She wrote to us every week and told us how happy you made her feel. That's why we wanted to meet you and tell you that you must come and stay with us anytime."

"I don't understand, Mrs Swithins," I whispered. "I don't understand what you're talking about."

Mrs Swithins took both my hands in hers and stared down at them.

"Robert is dead, Nancy. He was drowned in the summer. He was fishing on the lake in a rowing boat. And Caroline –" She looked up. "And Caroline won't accept it."

Mrs Swithins spoke as if she could hardly breathe. "No one can understand why she isn't getting better. We've spoken to Matron and she doesn't know. Then our doctor suggested we ask her best friend at school."

Mrs Swithins' eyes held mine. "Nancy, Caroline writes to us every week as if Robert's still alive. Do you have any idea why?"

Everything inside my head exploded like a firework.

I thought my heart would break.

Twelve

We sat in a corner in the rocks watching the sea crash over the pebbles. The water turned iron grey, then silver, as thin clouds flitted across a pale December sun. It was cold but we'd lit our fire in a sheltered place so it wasn't windy.

I pulled my brown woolly dress down over my knees and breathed in the smoky smell of sausages cooking.

"Almost ready," said Miss Parkes. "Are you hungry?"

Her short black hair stood on end and her face was red from the heat of the fire.

"You'd never believe I was a Girl Guide once, would you?"

I tried to smile. It felt a bit strange but it was good to be on the beach and hear the pebbles whooshing and clattering in the waves.

Miss Parkes picked up a bun and levered in a sausage from the frying pan.

"Ketchup?"

"Yes, please."

She wrapped it in a green school napkin and passed it over to me. Then she made one for herself and sat down beside me.

Neither of us spoke. I didn't know what to say. From the moment she had appeared in front of me at the hotel in Eastbourne, everything had happened in slow motion. And it was as if it was happening to someone else, not to me.

I had watched as Miss Parkes handed Mrs Swithins a letter. Somewhere in a big echoey cave, I heard her speak. She was sorry to cause any more pain in what she knew was a desperately sad situation. If Mrs Swithins would read the letter, she would understand everything.

Then Miss Parkes held out her hand to me and led me out of the hotel and onto the seafront.

The sausage was hot inside the napkin. I cupped it in my hand and stared out at the sea. Somewhere I knew I wanted to ask Miss Parkes lots of questions, but my head was full of fog. I couldn't find the words. I couldn't even see them clearly.

"Shall I tell you something about me?" said Miss

Parkes. She bit into her sausage and wiped a dribble of ketchup off her chin.

"Don't let your sausage get cold."

"No."

"I've never taught in a school before," said Miss Parkes with her mouth full. "I only left university this year. But I wanted to be a teacher, so when I saw the advertisement for a student teacher at Woodmaston House, I thought I'd give it a try."

She took another bite of her sausage. "When I came for my interview, they told me about your scholarship. They said I would be teaching you." She paused. "How's your sausage?"

"Very good, thanks."

"But when I arrived at the school," said Miss Parkes. "Everything was different. I found out that a lot of the things they told me at my interview weren't exactly true." She smiled at me. "Like teaching you, for a start."

I looked at her. There was something I wanted to ask her, but I couldn't remember what it was.

Miss Parkes patted my hand as if she knew what I was thinking. "Another sausage?"

"Yes, please." I'd eaten mine without even noticing.

She slid the sausages out of the pan into the buns. This time she did two together.

"Ketchup?"

"Yes, please."

I bit into my sausage and let the sweet greasy taste spread through me.

Little by little, the fog was lifting in my mind. For the first time since we'd left the hotel, I felt like it was me sitting on the beach and me eating a sausage. Not as if it was happening to someone else who looked like me but wasn't really there.

"Why didn't anyone tell me about Robert?" I whispered.

Miss Parkes moved close beside me and put her arm around my shoulder.

"Because no one understood how much it mattered," said Miss Parkes gently. "No one knew you made up wonderful stories about Robert for Caroline, except Jenny, Rosalind and Sharon. And no one knew that those stories kept him alive for her."

Miss Parkes squeezed my shoulder. "And I would

never have known if Jenny hadn't told me."

A long shudder went through me.

"I was so sad, Miss Parkes. You see, I thought about him all the time, too." I shook my head. "I know it sounds crazy now but felt I knew him and I was so close to him and I wanted to meet him more than anything."

"Jenny knew it was like that," said Miss Parkes, gently. "Though she made me promise not to tell." She smiled. "Nothing gets past your friend, Jenny. And nothing gets past me either."

Tears filled my eyes. "I don't know what I would have done if you hadn't come to the san last night."

Miss Parkes took my hand and held it. "I'm sorry, Nancy," she whispered. "Nothing like this should ever have happened."

"Are they going to send Nurse Blessed to prison?"

"I don't think so," said Miss Parkes. "But I don't know. You see, I've resigned from the school. That's why I wasn't in my room."

"Don't you want to be a teacher any more?"

Miss Parkes shook her head sadly. "Not for a while. I've decided to go back to university."

I watched the frothy edge of a wave seep into the pebbles and disappear. "Can I write to you?"

Miss Parkes leaned over and kissed my forehead. "Promise me?"

"I promise."

"Bloody hell, Nance," said Jenny from the other side of the dormitory. "I mean, who'd have ever thought this would happen?"

It was dark but the street lights and the three-quarters moon lit up the room.

All the beds were empty except two.

"I'm not having this crap," said Jenny. She jumped out of her own bed and shoved aside Caroline's empty bed, which was next to mine. It screeched across the floor but no one came in to tell us off.

"Here, give me a hand."

Between us, we pushed Jenny's bed across the floor so that it was beside mine. Once again there was a terrible noise but no one came in to stop us.

We lay in the shadowy light and held hands.

"It's sad about Bigfoot," said Jenny. She squeezed my hand. "I mean, I never thought for a moment –"

"Nor did I," I said.

"Jenny?"

"Yeah."

"Do you think my stories made her sick?"

"Nope. I think they made her happy. And I think if you hadn't told her those stories, they still wouldn't know how sick she is. So she can only get better." She paused. "Especially since she's out of this place."

"That's what Miss Parkes said."

"Then hey, kid," said Jenny in her terrible Texan drawl. "You'd better believe it."

"Jenny?"

"Yup."

"Is this school worse than the other schools you've been to?"

Jenny thought for a moment. "Well, I've only been to two, and at first I thought third time lucky. But you know, the truth is, Nance, this place takes the biscuit. It's a real dump."

I watched the branches of the monkey puzzle tree sway slowly in the breeze. Across the room, the praying hands turned silver in the moonlight. For the first time for ages, I thought about my red squirrel's foot and how Matron had so nearly found it. Maybe it wasn't a good luck charm after all. Maybe it would have been better if she'd chucked it away.

"Nance, honey?"

Back came the Texan drawl.

"Yeah?"

"I know this is real thoughtless and selfish an' all, what with all the terrible disasters and stuff –"

"Yeah."

"But would you gimme just one more ever lovin' story about me and the King?"

I could feel a grin spreading from my head all the way down to my feet.

"What's it to be, Jenny? "

"Nance, darlin'," drawled Jenny. "Ah just know that Elvis misses me so much he wants me outta here as fast as possible."

The air shuddered as something that looked like an enormous gold dragonfly landed on the playing fields. A silver crown glittered on its tail. A huge red E was painted on the door.

Jenny stood on the grass. A purple chiffon scarf

fluttered at her neck. She held down the shiny black dress that billowed around her thighs.

The door slid open and Elvis the King stood on the steps.

Jenny was ready for him. Only this time, things were a little bit different. She had a friend with her and her friend had a very important request.

Jenny stood on tiptoes and whispered into Elvis's ear.

"No problem, sweetheart," said the King. He turned to me and flashed a huge white smile.

"Okay, little lady. What can I do for you?"

I looked into Elvis's big brown eyes. "Does this thing carry lots of gas?"

"Thousands a' gallons, honey. Where do you wanna go?"

"Home," I said and I followed Jenny up the steps.

About the Author

Karen Wallace was born in Quebec and came to England in her early teens. She now lives in Herefordshire with her husband. Karen is the author of over 80 books for children, including her two novels: RASPBERRIES ON THE YANGTZE (Shortlisted for the Guardian Fiction Award) and CLIMBING A MONKEY PUZZLE TREE (Sunday Times Book of the Week), for both of which the inspiration and beautifully crafted backdrop came from her own childhood.

Wendy

KAREN WALLACE

Wendy

"Clever and original... this does something quite unexpected with Peter Pan" The Sunday Times

In a bold and unforgettable novel inpsired by the world of Peter Pan, Karen Wallace exposes the hypocrisy and cruelty behind the glittering facade of Edwardian London.

Wendy Darling endures the restricted life of a child born to a well-to-do Edwardian family. Confined to the nursery upstairs, she must protect her brothers from the vicious tricks of their cruel nanny. The glamour of her parents' parties downstairs calls to her and, risking punishment, she sneaks out at night to spy on grown-up life through the banisters. What she sees will change her life forever. The world beyond the nursery is haunted by secrets and passions that Wendy just can't fathom. Driven by her precocious imagination, Wendy sets out on a series of adventures to put the world about her to rights.

ISBN 0 689 83748 8

Raspberries on the Yangtze

"Can a book be funny, perceptive, moving and
utterly absorbing at one and the same time?
This one can. Brilliant.
A *'Swallows and Amazons'* for the 21st century."

Michael Morpurgo

ISBN: 0 689 83699 6